Viking Library System
1915 Fir Ave West
WITHDRAWN
218-739-5286
www.viking.lib.mn.us

Mercy Shot . . .

One of the patients was a woman holding a long knife with a curved blade that could have been used for filleting. She stared at Clint for a second before charging at him, knife gripped in both hands.

Clint could see the wild desperation in her eyes. The only time he'd seen anything like it was when people would spend so much time in an opium den that they were chased out of it by their own demons. When Clint raised his gun, he was doubly careful to take proper aim before pulling his trigger.

The Colt barked once and sent a round through the air that clipped the woman through the meat of her leg just above the knee. She spun around and toppled to the floor, even as she was still screaming and swinging her knife . . .

DON'T MISS THESE
ALL-ACTION WESTERN SERIES
FROM THE BERKLEY PUBLISHING GROUP

Viking Library System
218-736-5389

THE GUNSMITH by J. R. Roberts
   Clint Adams was a legend among lawmen, outlaws, and
   ladies. They called him . . . the Gunsmith.

LONGARM by Tabor Evans
   The popular long-running series about Deputy U.S. Marshal
   Custis Long—his life, his loves, his fight for justice.

SLOCUM by Jake Logan
   Today's longest-running action Western. John Slocum rides a
   deadly trail of hot blood and cold steel.

BUSHWHACKERS by B. J. Lanagan
   An action-packed series by the creators of Longarm! The
   rousing adventures of the most brutal gang of cutthroats ever
   assembled—Quantrill's Raiders.

DIAMONDBACK by Guy Brewer
   Dex Yancey is Diamondback, a Southern gentleman turned
   con man when his brother cheats him out of the family for-
   tune. Ladies love him. Gamblers hate him. But nobody pulls
   one over on Dex . . .

WILDGUN by Jack Hanson
   The blazing adventures of mountain man Will Barlow—from
   the creators of Longarm!

TEXAS TRACKER by Tom Calhoun
   J. T. Law: the most relentless—and dangerous—manhunter in
   all Texas. Where sheriffs and posses fail, he's the best man to
   bring in the most vicious outlaws—for a price.

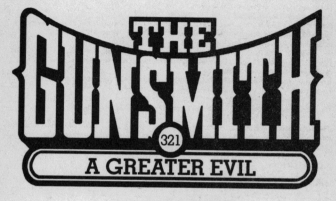

THE GUNSMITH

321

A GREATER EVIL

J. R. ROBERTS

JOVE BOOKS, NEW YORK

THE BERKLEY PUBLISHING GROUP
Published by the Penguin Group
Penguin Group (USA) Inc.
375 Hudson Street, New York, New York 10014, USA
Penguin Group (Canada), 90 Eglinton Avenue East, Suite 700, Toronto, Ontario M4P 2Y3, Canada
(a division of Pearson Penguin Canada Inc.)
Penguin Books Ltd., 80 Strand, London WC2R 0RL, England
Penguin Group Ireland, 25 St. Stephen's Green, Dublin 2, Ireland (a division of Penguin Books Ltd.)
Penguin Group (Australia), 250 Camberwell Road, Camberwell, Victoria 3124, Australia
(a division of Pearson Australia Group Pty. Ltd.)
Penguin Books India Pvt. Ltd., 11 Community Centre, Panchsheel Park, New Delhi—110 017, India
Penguin Group (NZ), 67 Apollo Drive, Rosedale, North Shore 0632, New Zealand
(a division of Pearson New Zealand Ltd.)
Penguin Books (South Africa) (Pty.) Ltd., 24 Sturdee Avenue, Rosebank, Johannesburg 2196,
South Africa

Penguin Books Ltd., Registered Offices: 80 Strand, London WC2R 0RL, England

This is a work of fiction. Names, characters, places, and incidents either are the product of the author's imagination or are used fictitiously, and any resemblance to actual persons, living or dead, business establishments, events, or locales is entirely coincidental.

A GREATER EVIL

A Jove Book / published by arrangement with the author

PRINTING HISTORY
Jove edition / September 2008

Copyright © 2008 by Robert J. Randisi.
Cover illustration by Sergio Giovine.

All rights reserved.
No part of this book may be reproduced, scanned, or distributed in any printed or electronic form without permission. Please do not participate in or encourage piracy of copyrighted materials in violation of the author's rights. Purchase only authorized editions.
For information, address: The Berkley Publishing Group,
a division of Penguin Group (USA) Inc.,
375 Hudson Street, New York, New York 10014.

ISBN: 978-0-515-14523-6

JOVE®
Jove Books are published by The Berkley Publishing Group,
a division of Penguin Group (USA) Inc.,
375 Hudson Street, New York, New York 10014.
JOVE is a registered trademark of Penguin Group (USA) Inc.
The "J" design is a trademark belonging to Penguin Group (USA) Inc.

PRINTED IN THE UNITED STATES OF AMERICA

10 9 8 7 6 5 4 3 2 1

If you purchased this book without a cover, you should be aware that this book is stolen property. It was reported as "unsold and destroyed" to the publisher, and neither the author nor the publisher has received any payment for this "stripped book."

ONE

The Colorado high country had just seen its first snow of the year. Thick layers of white covered the ground and were blown about by a stiff wind. It was just cold enough to keep the snow from melting, but not quite cold enough to freeze the breath inside a man's chest. That would come later. For the moment, Clint savored the chill and pulled in a deep lungful of the clean mountain air.

Eclipse shifted his hooves in the snow. The Darley Arabian stallion fussed a bit, but only because he was obeying Clint's wish to stand still for a bit longer than he would have wanted.

"What's the matter, boy?" Clint asked. "After all this riding, the cold finally catching up to you?"

If Eclipse could have replied with words, they wouldn't have been kind ones. That much was obvious by the loud snort that came from him amid a puff of steam from his nostrils.

Clint reached out to rub the side of Eclipse's neck, but winced and stopped short. The smile that had come to his face was quickly replaced by a grimace that showed more annoyance than pain. Even though it hurt him to do so, Clint stretched out his arm and scratched his stallion's ear.

Eclipse didn't seem to appreciate Clint's effort, since he continued to fret.

Snapping the reins, Clint pointed Eclipse's nose back to the trail he'd been following and let the Darley Arabian run as quickly as he pleased. At that moment, even the scent of evergreens didn't bring the smile back to Clint's face. All he wanted to do was to find the town called Running Springs, and he wanted to find it before the sun went down.

Unlike a ride over open country, plodding along mountain passes wasn't a time for speed. It was a chance for a horse and rider to put their skills to the test. One overly anxious snap of the reins could send both of them toppling along a jagged rock face or sliding into the middle of a frozen lake. Going too slowly, on the other hand, meant camping in the cold instead of in a room with a fire and wool blankets. At the very worst, it could mean freezing in the middle of a snowstorm that had dropped down from nowhere.

But Clint didn't have to worry about such things anymore. As soon as he spotted the black smoke hanging in the air, he traced it back to the chimneys that had created it and found a collection of buildings huddled together to form a small town. The sign posted outside the town was a welcome sight indeed. It bore the words Clint had been waiting to read: WELCOME TO RUNNING SPRINGS.

It was a good-size town that was fairly quiet. Then again, it could have been the sort of quiet that a cold snap always brought about. When there was enough snow on the ground and a harsh enough chill in the air, it took more than usual to break the silence. Every sound that was up to the task cracked through the air like a pike through a layer of ice. Clint found his eyes twitching back and forth in response to every clang of a hammer or slam of a door.

There seemed to be plenty of hotels in sight. In fact,

there seemed to be more than the normal number of hotels one might expect for a town of that size. There was also a generous helping of restaurants and saloons. It was a bit early in the day for the drinking halls to be too rowdy, so just about every storefront was as quiet as another. Clint brought Eclipse to a stop in front of a place with a large chimney and swung down from his saddle.

Sure enough, the first thing Clint saw when he stepped into the saloon was a huge, roaring fireplace. The mantel was only slightly shorter than the bar and the flames beneath it gave off enough heat to ease the chill that had seeped all the way down to the last drop of Clint's blood. After rubbing his hands in front of the fire for a few seconds, Clint turned toward the bar.

"Care for something to help with the cold, mister?" a barkeep with a thick, impeccably waxed mustache asked.

The barkeep's smile filled up all the space beneath his mustache, so it was hard for Clint not to return it. "No," Clint replied, "but I'd like something to help with the heat."

"I got just what you need." Reaching down to bring a bottle up from beneath the bar, the barkeep filled a small glass with whiskey and scooted it to the edge of the polished wooden surface. "One dose of heat, just what the doctor ordered."

Normally, Clint didn't drink whiskey. When he tossed the liquor down and swallowed it in one gulp, he considered it more of a way to thaw himself from the inside out than just taking a drink of whiskey. It didn't hurt that the whiskey was some of the smoothest he'd ever tasted.

"Not bad," Clint said as he set the glass down.

"Care for another?"

"How about some coffee?" Clint asked.

The barkeep kept his smile in place and put the bottle away. "Coming right up. You been in town long?"

"Just got here."

"What brings you to Running Springs?"

"Something you mentioned a bit earlier," Clint said.

That caught the barkeep off guard, and he froze with a mug in one hand and a coffeepot in the other. As the barkeep mulled through his thoughts, steam from the coffeepot rose up and drifted around his face. Finally, the barkeep had to shrug and admit, "Must have let my mouth run off on its own again. It has a tendency to do that."

"Doctor's orders," Clint said.

"Ah! You're here for . . ." The barkeep's sentence drifted off as his eyes took on a more cautious glint. "You're here to check into the sanitarium?"

"Just to visit," Clint amended. "I don't intend on staying for long. Does Dr. Wolcott still practice there?"

"Far as I know."

"Good. I require the services of a good physician and the only ones I've found recently reach their limits at tying off a bandage."

The relief was plain enough to see on the barkeep's face. He nodded and resumed filling the mug with hot coffee. "I got ya. For a moment, I thought you might be one of the loons that come here to check into the sanitarium for good. Then again, most of them fellas are escorted by someone with a badge and more than a few guns."

Clint picked up the mug and took a sip. Since the coffee was just fine on its own, he didn't bother asking for anything to add to it. "Some dangerous men are kept there?" he asked.

"Dangerous, sure, but also crazy as the day is long. This time of year, the day ain't too long, but you know what I mean."

"Yeah, I suppose I do."

"What sort of work you looking to have done over there?"

Rather than get into the entire story, Clint moved his

right arm as if he were slowly working out a kink. "Piece of metal got to a spot where it shouldn't be."

That seemed to be enough to satisfy the barkeep's curiosity. Either that, or he could tell Clint didn't want to get into the particulars. Either way, the other man let it go with a nod and consoling frown. "Might be a bit late to get your work done tonight. Rozekiel Sanitarium ain't that far from here, but it'll be locked up tight as a drum by the time you get out there. I don't know about contacting Dr. Wolcott. He lives on the other side of town."

"You know a warm place for me to spend the night?"

"That depends," the barkeep replied with a sly grin, "on what kind of warmth you're talkin' about. The Tall Pine Lodge has real cozy rooms, or Miss Connie's place one street over has a few girls that would melt the snow off the Rockies."

"The Tall Pine sounds good enough for now."

TWO

The Tall Pine Lodge was a little place with only four rooms available for rent. Although these were the more expensive rooms, they all came equipped with a coal stove in the middle of the floor that was meant more for giving off heat than any sort of cooking. Since Clint didn't have any meals to prepare, he was perfectly happy with the accommodations.

After a small meal of beef stew and wheat bread in the lodge's restaurant, he slipped under several layers of blankets and quilts for a good night's sleep. At least, it was as good a night's sleep as he could expect, considering the condition that had brought him to Colorado in the first place.

When the first rays of dawn crept into his room, Clint rolled onto his side and sucked in a quick breath as pain lanced through his right shoulder. He swung his legs over the side of the bed and rubbed the wound on his shoulder, which was already wrapped in several layers of bandages. While shuffling over to his washbasin, Clint removed the bandages and got a look at the wound.

"Damned Missouri sons of—" His grumbled curse was cut short when he poked the wrong spot on his shoulder and felt something like a small animal biting him from the inside. Clint gritted his teeth and kept prodding. One of the doctors he'd seen about the wound cautioned him to keep an eye out for any sign that it might be festering. So far, things didn't look that bad.

It hurt like hell, to be sure, but not as bad as it could.

Letting out the breath he'd been holding, Clint focused his eyes on the little iron stove directly in front of him. Once he'd stopped poking the wound and concentrated on the lettering stamped into the stove's door, he felt the pain start to ease somewhat. After a while, he felt the warmth of the stove that had soaked into the floorboards touch his feet and that took his mind away from his pain even more.

If the wound had been in any other spot, Clint would have been tempted to let any of the other doctors he'd seen try their hand at stitching him up. Even though Clint was no physician, he knew well enough that a chunk of lead in the wrong spot could do a whole lot of damage. He also knew that a pair of surgical tongs in the wrong set of hands could do even more damage.

The wound was to the shoulder of his gun arm, and it was close enough to his gun arm to jeopardize the speed of his draw. Any more damage could set him up for a real nice fall if some gunman with high aspirations decided to make a name for himself. Just because the Gunsmith wasn't at his best wouldn't stop such a man from taking a shot at bringing him down.

So far, Clint had been able to avoid trouble getting to Running Springs. If he needed to fight, he knew he could do a better job than most. Still, he wasn't about to take chances on doing anything that might hinder his ability for any more time than what was necessary. Just to gauge himself, Clint strapped his gun belt around his waist and took a few steps in front of his bed to get his blood flowing.

The modified Colt hung at his side in much the same way that his arm hung from his shoulder. The weight was so much a part of him that he barely even noticed it was there. If it weren't there, he would have felt like something less than a whole.

After setting his feet, Clint snapped his hand down to draw the Colt. Although his arm started to move with its normal speed, it was slowed by a pain that shot all the way down from the wound in his shoulder like a jagged bolt of lightning that extended to the ends of his fingers. His hand closed around the Colt, but he stopped it there.

Too slow.

Faster than most men could ever accomplish, but too slow for Clint's liking.

It wasn't the pain that kept Clint from drawing as quickly as he could. He'd felt plenty of pain throughout the years and he knew he'd feel plenty more. Sometimes, he could move faster and go farther than he'd ever thought he could when he was feeling the worst pain.

What slowed him down was the lead that was wedged into his flesh somewhere within his shoulder. It slowed him down like a thorn snagging his shirt every time he moved that arm. Normally, he could pull the thorn through and keep going just fine. At times when every split second counted, however, a snag like that could cost Clint his life.

Fixing his gaze upon a spot on the wall, Clint flexed his fingers and relaxed his arm. He took his eyes away from the wall, brought them up again, and then reached for his gun.

The familiar pain nipped into his muscles and then sunk into his arm like a hook at the end of a fishing line. Before he blinked again, his Colt was in his hand and he aimed at the spot on the wall. If he pulled his trigger, he knew he could put a round through that very spot.

That wasn't the problem.

His draw was still slow. He could have probably gotten the drop on close to three-quarters of the men he might meet, but Clint wasn't about to bet on avoiding that other quarter. He dropped the gun back into its place at his side and then quickly pulled on the rest of his clothes.

Coffee was being brewed within the hotel somewhere and it smelled even better than the brew that was served at the saloon the night before. Clint could also pick out the scent of something baking, which might have been biscuits or some kind of griddle cake. He'd smelled better, but his stomach was grumbling and there were surely plenty of other breakfasts being whipped up elsewhere in town. Clint made himself presentable so he could claim one of those breakfasts for himself.

THREE

After filling his belly with flapjacks and strong coffee, Clint followed the directions he'd been given that lead him out of the town's limits and to the place called Rozekiel Sanitarium. Although the trail leading to the place took him through some thick woods, Clint didn't have any trouble spotting the large structure, which seemed to be built into the side of an even larger hill.

Rozekiel looked like it had started off as a mansion, but had been modified to suit the needs of the doctors who had come along to inhabit it. A sign the size of an overturned kitchen table was at the end of a path that led from the trail and went all the way up to the sanitarium's front door. That sign had the look of freshly carved wood and spelled Rozekiel Sanitarium in solid block lettering.

Taking his time to ride along the winding path, Clint got a good look at the place. It seemed as if every room had its own small windows because the square panes of glass formed three neat rows that appeared to go all the way around the building. The front of the building may have been pretty at one time or another, but it wasn't much to look at anymore. This didn't appear to be from a lack of upkeep, but instead the result of bad decisions on the part of the groundskeeper. The shrubs along the front were cut low. The front door was plain and thick. When he dismounted and led Eclipse by the reins, Clint could tell some sort of decoration around the entryway had been removed.

Before Clint got close enough to climb the two steps leading to the front door, he saw the door open and two people come outside. One of them was a man in his late forties with a full beard and the other was a boy who immediately ran toward Eclipse.

"Welcome to Rozekiel Sanitarium," the man declared. "Are you here to visit someone, or is this a business matter?"

"I'm here to see Dr. Wolcott," Clint replied.

"Is he expecting you?"

"No, but a friend of his in Kansas recommended that I see him."

The man nodded and obviously chose his words carefully when he asked, "Are you having difficulties or is this concerning a family member?"

It was only then that Clint noticed another sign embedded into the front of the building, just to the right of the entrance and mostly hidden in shadow. It was a plaque that read: ROZEKIEL ASYLUM.

"It's about me, but it's just an injury," Clint replied. He was quick to add, "An injury in my shoulder. Not in my head. At least . . . not the sort that someone in a place like this would—"

The other man held up his hands and said, "No need to explain. Dr. Wolcott is a renowned surgeon and he still gets his occasional patient from that discipline."

"If that means he still stitches up flesh wounds, then that's good news for me," Clint said.

"He does. I'm Dr. Liam, by the way."

"Clint Adams."

As Dr. Liam shook Clint's hand, he said, "Patrick will take your horse to our stable in the back. Is that all right?"

"Sure. Just make sure he's easy on the greens."

Patrick was in a rush to get over to Eclipse, but slowed down to a careful, deliberate pace the moment he got close enough to rub the stallion's nose. He was a skinny kid with an earnest face that looked slightly afraid when he got a look at the gun hanging at Clint's side. "All right, mister," he said. "I'll even brush him for you. I'll do a real good job."

"Be sure that you do," Clint said sternly. "That way I'll know you earned this." With that, Clint flipped a silver dollar through the air.

Patrick caught the dollar in both hands. When he looked down at what he had, he was so surprised that he nearly dropped it. "Yes, sir!" he said as if he were about to salute. "I'll do a real good job."

Eclipse followed the boy without fussing. Since the Darley Arabian seemed to trust Patrick, Clint didn't have any reservations about the kid. He watched Patrick lead Eclipse away as Clint himself was led to the front door by Dr. Liam.

"Seems like your signs don't match," Clint pointed out as he nodded toward the mostly obscured plaque hanging next to the front door.

Dr. Liam spared half a glance toward the plaque and pushed open the front door. "Oh, that's a holdover from when Rozekiel first opened its doors to patients. Places like asylums from years past seem like dungeons in comparison to our new philosophy. In recent years, we've been trying to treat our patients as good people who need care, not as prisoners."

"I hope some of the dangerous folks aren't allowed to come and go as they please," Clint said.

"We take the necessary precautions when needed."

As Clint walked through the main entrance, he found himself in a small foyer that looked like the front desk of a fancy hotel. There was a clerk sitting behind a large counter, surrounded by stacks of ledgers and papers of all sizes. The clerk glanced up just long enough to see a familiar face and then quickly got back to his work.

"So what brings you to Rozekiel?" Dr. Liam asked.

Just hearing that question brought a painful twitch to Clint's shoulder. "I caught some lead in Kansas."

"Oh my! You were shot?" Dr. Liam asked as he walked past the front desk and led Clint down a hallway.

There had been plenty of lead flying at the time, but Clint didn't feel like getting into all the details. Instead, he gave the short version. "More of a ricochet, I think. It's not bad enough to be a full gunshot wound, but there's some lead in my shoulder."

"Weren't there any doctors in Kansas?"

"Sure, and a few of them seemed more than willing to dig around in my arm to pull the lead out. They said there was a good chance I'd lose some of the use of it or might even have one or two fingers go numb, but they were eager to have some practice in doing the procedure."

"Ahh," Dr. Liam said sympathetically. "I see."

"I've been meaning to head into the Rockies for some time, and a friend of mine said that Dr. Wolcott could probably get this lead out of me without a hitch, so I thought I'd pay him a visit."

"Well, you've made an excellent choice," Dr. Liam declared. They'd walked almost to the end of the hall and still had yet to pass one door that looked different from all the others. Every last door was the same height, made of the same color wood, and held in place by the same brass hinges. As far as Clint could tell, there wasn't one nail pounded into the wall and no hint of anything as simple as a picture or a vase of flowers to add some color to the place.

Dr. Liam kept his friendly smile in place and kept

speaking in a cheery tone. "Dr. Wolcott once removed a bullet from a man's hip and gave him full use of his legs when other doctors swore the man wouldn't be able to walk without a cane for the rest of his life."

"I heard that same story," Clint said. "In fact, that man is the one who pointed me in this direction."

Dr. Liam's eyes brightened as he looked over at Clint again. "How is Jacob doing?"

"Just fine. I think he could beat me in a footrace."

"Excellent. You can wait for Dr. Wolcott in there."

Clint looked at the door that Dr. Liam was pointing to and found it to be just another one in the plain row of look-alikes. "If this is a bad time, I could always come back."

"We're all going to be busy no matter when anyone comes calling. An appointment wouldn't change that."

"All right, then. Should I just wait inside?"

Pushing the door open a bit more, Dr. Liam nodded. "Make yourself comfortable."

One glance into the room was enough to convince Clint he wouldn't be comfortable in that room even if it were padded with down feathers. The walls were perfectly straight and barren, except for a single framed document above a small rectangular table. That table must have been a desk, because it had a few stacks of papers and a few pens on it, but lacked anything more personal than that. For all Clint knew, the stack could be lists of supplies ordered by the place's kitchen. There were three chairs in the room, all of which were of an identical, straight-backed design that looked better suited to hold more stacks of papers.

"That's all right," Clint said. "I can just—"

"Nonsense," Dr. Liam said as he all but shoved Clint into the room. "You wait here just a few minutes and Dr. Wolcott will be right with you."

Before Clint could protest any further, Dr. Liam stepped

back and shut the door between them. Once the door's latch fell into place, Clint couldn't help but feel as if he'd been captured by the imposing structure of the sanitarium and couldn't leave no matter how much he wanted to go.

FOUR

Clint was kept waiting just long enough to think about sneaking out of the building altogether. Before he could open the door and take his chances in the hallway, the door was opened by a tall man with a stocky build dressed in a long white coat. His round face was clean shaven and his brown hair only grew in a ring around the back of his head, leaving the top of his head shiny and bald.

"Hello, there," the tall man said. "Are you Clint Adams?"

"I am."

"I'm Dr. Wolcott. What seems to be your trouble?"

Still standing and contemplating his escape, Clint quickly replied, "I've got a wound in my shoulder, but it's not so bad."

"My colleague tells me you came all the way from Kansas. Are you a friend of Jacob's?"

"Yes."

"He's still getting himself into trouble, I take it?"

Perhaps it was the doctor's kind voice or the fact that the man was big enough to completely block the doorway, but Clint stopped thinking about running away. Instead, he removed his jacket and showed the doctor his bandaged shoulder.

"Jacob and I were riding in a posse together in western Kansas," Clint said. "Some robbers were holed up in a cave and started shooting. We got them out, but not until a lot of lead was let loose. Most of those bullets wound up bouncing off the cave walls and a piece of one wound up in my shoulder."

Wolcott had already peeled back Clint's bandages and was examining the wound underneath them. His brow was furrowed and his eyes were narrowed into intense slits. "This is very close to some important ligaments."

"I know. I don't know the medical terms for it, but I can feel something scraping against something that's awfully tender. Since my fingers have been going numb every now and then, I figured I needed someone better than a prairie doctor to dig around in there. Jacob said you were just the man for the job."

"And he was right," Wolcott said with a confident smile. "I can take some time right now, if you like."

"I can come back if it suits you," Clint offered. "I've waited this long."

"Which is exactly why you shouldn't wait any longer. Come with me and I'll take you to another room where I can get that lead out of you."

Even though he was afraid of what answer he might get, Clint asked, "Will I lose any use of my arm?"

"Looks like you've been using it pretty well so far. Hopefully, I won't make things any worse for you."

Clint followed the doctor through another maze of hallways that led to a narrow staircase. It was no surprise that there was yet another hallway at the top of those stairs. The only difference between that one and the hall on the lower floor was that there was even less space to move about. As hard as that was to believe, Clint soon realized that there was no lobby at the end of this hall and none of those windows he saw from the outside were visible at the moment.

"Most of these are rooms where we work on our patients," Wolcott said. Pushing open one of the doors and waving inside, he added, "Step right in there and make yourself comfortable."

The room had a few stools that were only slightly better than something used for milking a cow. They were positioned around a small examining table and a straight-backed chair. Clint draped his jacket over the back of the chair and unbuttoned his shirt. "You need to get a better look at the wound?" he asked.

"Already got all the look I need," Wolcott said. "I assume you're anxious to get that lead out of you. Besides, you just happened to catch me before one of my sessions with the patients on the third floor."

"If this is a bad time—"

"They can wait a bit. Changing the schedule every now and then keeps them on their toes. Since I don't allow myself to be interrupted during my sessions, catching me in between them is your only hope. Since we're both here now, let's just get this done."

While letting out a breath and taking off his shirt, Clint sat in the chair and sighed. "Amen to that."

Within seconds of getting his shirt off, Clint saw someone walking down the hall toward his room. Given how quiet the entire building seemed to be, Clint was surprised to spot another person moving inside the place.

The person in the hall was a tall, slender woman with long, straight blond hair that was pulled back into a tail and held in place by a green ribbon. She had a pleasant smile on her face, which quickly turned into an embarrassed wince when she got a look at Clint's bare chest.

"Oh," she said. "I'm sorry. I was just looking for Dr. Wolcott."

Wolcott rolled up his sleeves and rummaged through some tools that were kept in a drawer. "You found me, Heather. What can I do for you?"

Shielding her eyes with one hand, Heather stretched out her other arm to offer some papers to the doctor. "Here are those files you asked for," she said in a nervous voice. "And, also, you're late for your session on the third floor."

"I'm aware of that, Heather. Thank you. Just leave those papers on the table."

Since she needed to look at what she was doing to keep from dropping the papers, Heather lowered her hand and stepped into the room to set them down. Once her eyes found Clint again, she wasn't quick to move them away. "Thank you," she said with a grin. Suddenly, her eyes darted to Wolcott and she straightened. "I mean, thank you, Doctor."

Wolcott turned to face Clint and shook his head. "Sorry about that. I don't know what's gotten into her."

Clint smirked as he watched Heather rush from the room. Her plain white dress hugged a trim, attractive body. He particularly enjoyed the sight of her little backside twitching as she bustled away.

FIVE

The third floor of Rozekiel Sanitarium looked a lot like the floors below it. There were more hallways, more barren walls, and more locked doors. The third floor did have a few things that the rest of the building didn't, however. That floor housed a man named Solomon Reyes. It also had a room that was filled with a whole lot of dead bodies.

Solomon was a bit shy of average height, but had enough muscle packed onto his frame to split the difference. His round head was covered with irregularly cut stubble that seemed equally spread along his scalp and face. The black whiskers gave his face a shadowy appearance, while the uneven clumps of hair on top of his head made him look like he'd been chewed up and spit out.

Pushing open one of the doors at the end of the hall with his hip, Solomon shuffled backward into the room while dragging the limp body of an orderly by the shoulders. The orderly was dressed in gray and his head hung at an odd angle when it wasn't lolling with every bump along the way. As soon as he was inside the room, Solomon tossed the orderly against the same wall as the rest of the bodies.

"It wasn't supposed to get this bad," Solomon said.

There was nobody else in the room with him. At least, there wasn't anyone in there who was able to respond. But Solomon didn't seem to expect a response, since he continued to mutter under his breath while straightening up the bodies.

"It was supposed to be quick and easy. Quick and easy," he said as he shuffled around the room to check all the faces of the dead men. Fixing his gaze upon the room's single, small square window, he grumbled, "Maybe I should just get out this way."

His thick hands slapped against the window, but didn't get it to move. Not only had the window been painted shut, but there also were four nails beneath the paint that were driven through the window's frame that kept it from budging. Solomon scraped away the paint with his fingers and immediately got to work on the nails. He didn't seem to feel anything as he dug and scraped at the nails. When the blood started to flow from his fingertips, he didn't seem to notice that, either.

He pried one nail up far enough to pull it from the wood and then loosened two more before he had enough slack to rip the window up from where it had been secured. All Solomon had to do was take a look outside to lose all the steam he'd built up to get it open. His eyes widened and he pulled in a quick breath.

"Bad idea," he whispered. "Too high. Much too high."

Solomon wheeled around to put his back against the window. His eyes darted over the bodies, but settled upon the door. He pulled in one breath after another, drawing more air with every gulp until he was finally able to steady himself enough to nod.

"I came this far. I can go the rest. I can walk right out of here."

With that, he stepped up to the door and pulled it open. Solomon leaned forward until he could get a look into the hallway. He spotted another group of men in white and gray coming down the hall, headed in his direction. More important, those men spotted him.

"There he is," the biggest of the orderlies said. After that, the whole group of them rushed toward Solomon's room.

"Can't walk out of here," Solomon said to himself. "Gotta run."

He was still muttering those words as he threw open the door, jumped out of the room, and bolted down the hall. His bare feet pounded against the clean wooden floor and scraped against the occasional raised nail. Leaning forward, Solomon put his weight behind his shoulder and aimed that shoulder at the gut of the closest orderly.

Even though the first orderly tried to brace himself against Solomon's charge, he still lost every bit of air from his lungs when he caught that shoulder in his midsection. Solomon drove into the orderly as if he meant to run straight through him. He felt a bit of resistance on impact, but pushed right through it until the orderly was down and sliding against the wall.

The second orderly wasn't as big as the first, but was more prepared for a fight. He gripped a club in one hand and swung it in a low arc that was meant to take Solomon out at the knees. At the last second, Solomon turned and caught the blow on the side of his legs instead. The club still did some damage, but not nearly as much as the orderly had intended.

Feeling the dull pain from the club that had pounded his thigh, Solomon gritted his teeth and kept running. He wanted to make the orderly sorry for hitting him, but he wanted to get to the stairs at the other end of the hall even more.

Solomon kept his sights set upon those stairs. He put every bit of strength he could muster into his legs as he raced down the hall. Because of that, he was caught unaware when a third orderly managed to catch up to him and tackle him at waist level.

A strong set of arms wrapped around Solomon's midsection and even managed to lift him off his feet. Solomon's legs continued to kick and his arms flailed as he was hauled up just enough to bring him to a halt. Now that he was no longer moving, Solomon put all of his efforts into getting free.

Without taking the time to look at who'd grabbed him, Solomon twisted around and swung his arm behind him. His elbow thumped against the orderly who'd grabbed him, so he pulled that arm back and hit the orderly again.

"Someone help me with this one before he gets away!" the orderly who held on to Solomon demanded.

The first orderly was still dragging himself up to his feet after being knocked down. The other two were both armed with clubs and rushed over to get close enough so they could use them.

Solomon was still unable to free himself from the grip of the orderly who'd brought him to a halt in the first place. Now that he was twisted around enough, he could see that the one who'd locked him in a bear hug was the same orderly who normally brought Solomon his meals at the beginning and end of each day. While they might have been friendly to each other before, Solomon didn't feel obliged to keep up that behavior any longer. Instead, Solomon tightened his fist and cracked his elbow against the side of the orderly's head. That got the other man to loosen his grip awfully quick.

Just as Solomon shoved the orderly aside, another orderly moved around to cut him off from the stairs. This orderly was an older fellow who also carried a club, and he wasn't afraid to put it to use. The club sliced through the air and landed against Solomon's ribs. Pain exploded through that side of Solomon's body, making it next to impossible for him to draw his next breath.

Solomon did his best to fight back, but could only land a punch or two before he felt the club slam against him one more time. Despite the throbbing agony that filled his battered body, Solomon lowered his arm and locked it as best he could to trap the orderly's club.

The orderly pulled, but wasn't quite strong enough to pull his club from between Solomon's arm and side. Solomon's fist cracked against the orderly's face, but only hard enough to snap the other man's head to one side for a second. It wasn't a strong enough blow to cause the terror that had suddenly appeared in the orderly's eyes. Solomon was certain it wasn't a hard enough punch to get the orderly to drop to one knee and give up the fight altogether.

Once the orderly had dropped, Solomon could see the other man standing behind him.

Wearing a smile that seemed to have been smeared onto his face by an overzealous painter, the man behind the orderly twisted the knife he'd buried into the orderly's spine and then viciously ripped it free. Behind him, another orderly was crumpled in a bloody heap, a third was writhing in agony, and the remaining one was running for his life in the opposite direction.

"Oh, no," Solomon whispered. "More bodies."

SIX

Clint grabbed on to the arm of his chair until he thought he might rip it off. He gritted his teeth and locked his eyes on to the square window in front of him as Dr. Wolcott continued to dig around in the fleshy part of his shoulder. When the doctor found the piece of lead that had been causing all the trouble, Clint could hear the crunch echo throughout his entire head.

"There we are," Wolcott said calmly. "Got the nasty little bugger."

Although Clint wanted to calmly request that the doctor hurry up, he knew his words wouldn't come out nearly as polite as he planned. Rather than spit out a string of obscenities, he kept his mouth shut and let Wolcott do his job.

Wolcott twisted the instrument in Clint's arm a bit more, dragged the broken metal through Clint's flesh, and then finally pulled it back. When everything was out of his arm, Clint was so relieved he wanted to get up and dance. Instead, he let out a long breath and allowed his head to droop forward.

"I'll bet that feels better," Wolcott said.

Before Clint could express his gratitude, the door to the room was pushed open and Heather rushed inside.

"I am almost finished with this man," Wolcott snapped as the lead piece hit the bottom of a tin pan with a loud *clank*. "Whatever the problem may be, I'm sure it can—"

"Four men were killed and some of the patients escaped!" Heather said.

Wolcott was frozen with one hand still holding his surgical tool over the tin pan. "What?"

"Four men are dead," she repeated. "More are hurt, but I don't know how many."

"Who escaped?"

"I don't know. They all came from the third floor."

"Good Lord." Wolcott sighed.

Clint leaned forward and reached for his shirt. Even that simple movement was enough to make the entire right half of his upper body feel like it was on fire. "What happened?" he asked groggily.

Heather looked at Clint for a second, but she was too frantic to look at any one spot for longer than that. "On the third floor! There's been—"

Cutting her short with an upraised hand, Wolcott stood up and said, "Just a little trouble among the patients," he snapped. "Nothing for you to concern yourself with, Mr. Adams."

"But if there've been men hurt I can . . ." Clint paused when he saw Wolcott try to stop him in the same way he'd cut Heather off. But Clint wasn't about to let himself be silenced so easily. "I might be able to help," Clint said deliberately.

Wolcott did a poor job of hiding his annoyance at being overruled that way. "We have orderlies for that purpose, Mr. Adams."

Suddenly, footsteps pounded against the floorboards and stomped up the nearby stairs. Overhead, more footsteps stampeded back and forth on the third floor.

Clint glanced up and said, "Sounds to me like your men could use some help."

But Wolcott was already up and heading for the door. "You're in no condition for this, Mr. Adams. After what you just went through, you need to catch your breath. You can sit here if you like, or you can stretch out in one of the beds in another room." Stepping into the hall and easing the door shut behind him, Wolcott added, "Some of our patients get overeager, but it's nothing to worry about. We are professionals here. We know what we are doing. Thank you very much."

With that, Wolcott stepped all the way out of the room and pulled the door shut until the latch fell into place. After exchanging some words with Heather, he and the blonde added their own footsteps to the noise filling the building.

Clint buttoned his shirt and stared at the door for a few seconds. Although his arm hurt worse than it had since he'd gotten the original wound, he could already feel a difference since the lead was out of him. He thought about the doctor's orders and eased back into his chair. As soon as he heard what could have been a man tripping down a flight of stairs, Clint jumped up and headed for the door.

"Professionals, my ass," Clint grumbled as he pulled open the door and ran toward the source of the most noise.

SEVEN

Clint barely made it to the end of the hall before he felt the blood starting to flow from the wound in his shoulder. Clint was surprised that it had started bleeding, since Dr. Wolcott had shored a heavy bandage on the wound before he left with Heather. Whatever had been done was quickly being undone, but Clint wasn't about to stop and turn back now.

Grabbing the first worker he could find, Clint asked, "What's going on here?"

"Someone's putting up a fight on the third floor," the young orderly replied. "I hear it's already gotten pretty bloody." Those last few words were shouted over his shoulder as he bounded up the stairs at the end of the hall.

Keeping his hand upon the grip of his holstered Colt, Clint followed the orderly up the steps and emerged on the next floor. If he hadn't known better, he might have thought he'd somehow wound up back on the second floor. The only thing that made this floor distinctive in the slightest was all the commotion within the drab hallway. A few men were lying along the edge of the hall, but most of the activity came from the men and women who ran up and down along the cramped corridor.

Clint picked out one young man at the end of the hall.

He set his sights on that one because he watched the young man stop and exchange a few words with plenty of others, including one of the fellows who seemed to be unable to get up and join the rest of the commotion. Once the young man was close enough, Clint snagged ahold of him by the arm and asked, "What's going on here?"

Immediately, the young man's eyes went down to the Colt at Clint's side. "Are you here to catch them?"

"I need to know what's going on before I can catch anyone."

"All I know is that Solomon Reyes and some others broke out of here and killed at least two guards along the way."

"Guards?" Clint asked.

The younger man squinted and took a closer look at Clint. "That's right. Don't you know about the third floor? Who are you?"

Before the younger man could become even more suspicious, Clint asked, "Who else was hurt?"

"We don't know yet. I was just about to check in the kitchen, since that's where Reyes is supposed to be holed up."

"Perfect," Clint said. "Lead the way."

Even though the younger man still had his reservations, seeing the gun at Clint's side went a long way to boost his confidence. He headed for the stairs and ran all the way down them with Clint on his heels. After reaching the bottom floor, the young man navigated to the back of the building until they finally reached a section that wasn't nearly identical to all the others.

"The kitchen's straight through there," the young man said as he pointed to a set of double doors at the other end of a large room that was filled with what looked to be several rows of picnic tables.

Although the dining room was fairly empty, Clint could

tell there were plenty of people nearby. He could hear them screaming. "How many men are we up against?" Clint asked.

"I don't know. We only know that they made a break for it. Could be four or five."

"Are they dangerous?"

The young man didn't even have to think about that one. "Yes. That's why they were on the third floor."

"Could they have guns?"

"I don't think so. Not even the guards carry guns. They all just carry clubs."

Upon hearing the clatter of dishes followed by another scream, Clint added, "There's got to be plenty of knives in there for them to use."

"Yeah," the young man said as the color drained from his face.

"Try to round up as many other guards as you can," Clint said. "Is there a way out of the building through the kitchen?"

"Yes!"

"Then get as many men as you can to go outside and cut off that escape route. I'll try to flush them out."

"What if . . . What if they come running back through here?" the young man asked in a way that made him seem afraid of the answer he might get.

"Then the rest of you men can catch them," Clint replied. "Wasn't that the plan all along?"

Rather than wait for the young man to pull together a response, Clint rushed through the dining room and placed his back against the wall next to the double doors. He pulled in a breath and did his best to ignore the pain coming from his aching shoulder. Since he wasn't sure about the speed of his draw, he took the Colt from its holster and held it down low as he shoved the door open with his good shoulder.

The kitchen was a mess of broken plates and panicked folks of all shapes and sizes. Pots and pans were scattered on the floor, tripping up people as they raced from one spot to another like chickens after their heads had been cut off. Clint was able to pick out most of the kitchen workers by the various uniforms they wore. Of course, the patients weren't exactly hard to miss, either.

"THE DEVIL LIVES HERE!!!" a man with long white hair screamed as he swung a meat cleaver at the back of a fleeing woman. Pointing to Clint, he shouted, "THERE HE IS!!!"

Hearing that, three more people dressed in rags similar to the ones the long-haired old man wore snapped their heads up and stared at Clint. Their clothes were light brown and hung on them as if each had been given the same set of cheaply made clothes poorly sewn to a single size and pattern. The smaller patients were swimming in the garments, while men like the fellow with the long hair looked more like boys who'd outgrown their britches years ago.

One of the patients was a woman, and she held a long knife with a curved handle that could have been used for filleting. The other two were hunkered down over a trio of small women who were dressed in white smocks and aprons common in any kitchen. The woman stared at Clint for a second before charging at him with her knife gripped in both hands.

Even though Clint had only seen those patients for a few seconds, he was able to pick out the wild desperation in their eyes. The only time he'd seen anything like it was when people would spend so much time in an opium den that they were chased out of it by their own demons. When Clint raised his gun, he was doubly careful to take proper aim before pulling his trigger.

The Colt barked once and sent a round through the air

that clipped the woman with the knife through the meat of her leg just above the knee. She spun around and toppled to the floor, even as she was still screaming and swinging her knife.

Clint's next two shots came in quick succession and whipped through the air over two of the frantic patients' heads. Although he could have gotten them closer with a few more seconds to aim, Clint didn't want to take any chances considering the wound in his gun arm. The two shots he fired were good enough to send the two patients scrambling for the back door as they let their weapons fall from their hands.

That left only the old man with the long hair and the meat cleaver. He stood his ground and puffed out his chest as if he were facing down his final judgment. "I DEFY YOU, SATAN!" he screamed. "And I do this in the NAME OF ALL THAT'S GOOD!!!!"

Clint didn't pay attention to any of the old man's words. Instead, he took that time to aim and squeeze his trigger. Just as the old man started to swing his cleaver at the closest living thing he could reach, Clint's modified Colt sent another round through the air.

The lead hissed across the kitchen, sparked against the large blade of the old man's cleaver, and buried itself into one of the nearby cabinets. The impact of the bullet was more than enough to take a large chip from the blade and pull the entire cleaver out of the old man's grasp.

As the cleaver rattled against the floor, the old man stared down at it with wide eyes. His mouth hung open in an expression of utter disbelief, which might have been comical if not for the situation that had led up to it. "Was that you, Barbory?" the old man whispered. "You want me to go to sleep now?"

Clint walked forward and motioned for the remaining workers to leave through the double doors behind him.

Since the old man didn't make a move for the cleaver and wasn't holding any other sort of weapon, Clint holstered the Colt and said, "Yeah. Maybe you should go to sleep."

The old man nodded and lay down on the floor. "I am awfully tired, Barbory."

EIGHT

Clint wasn't sure if the young orderly had followed the orders he'd been given or if the Rozekiel guards did it on their own, but there was a large reception committee waiting outside to catch the patients who bolted out the kitchen's back door. More of the burly men came into the kitchen wielding clubs to collect the old man. Clint stepped back and let the guards do their work. Somewhere along the line, he realized his wound was bleeding again.

Dr. Liam rushed around on the first floor like a worker ant and raced toward Clint the moment he spotted him. "You're bleeding! Did one of them hurt you?"

"No," Clint replied. "That's just my wound that needs stitching."

"Oh, right. I can stitch you up."

Waving off the doctor's advances, Clint said, "It's nice of you to offer, but you folks have got your hands full here. There should be a doctor in Running Springs that can sew me up."

"Are you sure?"

"Oh, yeah. Is everything under control here?"

Liam nodded. "There's wounded to tend to, but the storm's over."

"Good to hear it. Just point me toward the front door and I'll be on my way."

Despite his willingness to help stop Clint's bleeding, Dr. Liam had plenty more to contend with. He showed Clint the way to the front lobby and then rushed off to lend a hand with one of the several other problems raging inside Rozekiel.

Clint left the building and stopped as soon as he was outside. Although he could still hear some of the commotion from inside as well as a few echoes from the back of the place, it was downright tranquil compared to the chaos he'd left behind.

There was a gentle breeze blowing in from the north and the cold was just crisp enough to soothe Clint's entire body rather than freeze him to the bone. Clint even took a moment to close his eyes and savor the way the cold air drifted beneath his clothes like a set of wandering fingers. When he opened his eyes again, he spotted a familiar face studying him from a distance.

"Is it over?" Patrick asked from his spot behind a shed just off the main path leading up to Rozekiel's front door.

Clint smiled at the stable boy and shook his head. "Not quite, but things are well in hand. You should stay out here for a while, though."

"I wasn't about to go inside," Patrick replied intensely. "Not with all them loons runnin' about."

"Are things safe in the stable?"

That brought an immediate grin to the kid's face. "Yes, sir. I guarded them horses myself."

"How about you take me to it?"

"Come on over!"

Clint followed the kid around the corner of the main

building until he spotted another structure that looked like a barn that had been cut in half and stretched out a bit. Although there obviously wasn't a loft, the stable was long enough to hold everything it needed as well as several horses. Patrick ran inside and motioned for Clint to keep up with him.

"I already brushed him and everything!" Patrick said as he proudly waved toward the stall where Eclipse was waiting.

Sure enough, the Darley Arabian looked more presentable than Clint himself and calmly chewed on some oats as the rest of the sanitarium raged nearby.

"You did a good job, Patrick. Does this sort of thing happen here a lot?"

"Sometimes," the kid replied. "But I just stay out here and hide in back. If any of them loons come to bother the horses, they usually get caught by one of the guards."

"This place has a lot of guards for a hospital," Clint mused.

"Not enough, if you ask me."

"Why do you say that?"

Patrick shifted on his feet and wrung his hands. Finally, he said, "There wasn't enough to keep the horses from gettin' stole today."

"There were horses stolen?" Clint asked.

"I think so. Either that, or some of the guards collected theirs to ride after one of them loons. I was hidin' in there when it happened," Patrick said as he pointed toward a large bin filled with blankets and grooming supplies. "Some guards rushed out sayin' they had to round up somebody."

"So it was guards that got their horses?"

Shrugging, Patrick nodded. "Yeah, I suppose. I was hidin'."

Clint glanced around and took note of the condition of the stable. Compared to what he'd seen inside the sanitarium, the stable was in perfect order. Even the empty stalls looked as if whatever animals had been there were taken out calmly by someone who was thinking clearly enough to shut the gate behind him.

"You did the right thing by hiding," Clint told the boy. "And you did a fine job with Eclipse."

"Should I go back inside?"

Even though the ruckus from the main building was dying down, Clint said, "You'd best keep your head down until someone comes out here to fetch you. Think you can do that?"

"Yes sir," Patrick replied. As soon as those words were out of him, the boy turned and started running toward his hiding spot. He paused halfway there and asked, "Are you leaving?"

"I sure am."

"You need help with his saddle?"

"No, thanks. I think I can manage."

Patrick waved and raced for his hiding place.

Although tightening the buckles on his saddle as well as climbing up into it strained his wound, Clint was happy to do it. He was even happier when he rode away from Rozekiel to let the doctors clean up their own mess.

NINE

Clint rode back into Running Springs with his jacket open so the cold wind could wrap around him. Not only was it refreshing after the stifling confines of Rozekiel Sanitarium, but the cold numbed his wound until he could only feel an occasional throb to remind him it was there. As much as he wanted to have something to eat or possibly even a drink, Clint rode past the saloons and restaurants until he found a doctor's office on the corner of Main Street.

The doctor was a sleepy-eyed fellow who shuffled as if he were walking through frozen sap. To his credit, the doctor didn't ask many questions and stitched up Clint with a steady hand. He accepted his fee graciously and then shuffled back to whatever he'd been doing before Clint had arrived.

Clint's stomach was just starting to grumble when he put Eclipse up in a stable that was close to his hotel, but he fought the urge to eat right away. There was a more pressing matter for him to attend to and he couldn't exactly do it around a lot of people.

Since Running Springs wasn't exactly a big town, Clint only needed to walk for a few minutes before he was on a footpath that led into a wooded area. Before much longer, he found what could have been the town's namesake, even though the springs weren't exactly running at the moment. It was frozen along the edges, making it quiet enough to hear the footsteps of some nearby squirrels.

Clint stood at the edge of the water, picked a tree across the spring, and then drew his Colt. The moment he cleared leather, he could tell his aim would be off. Sure enough, his bullet flew a little right of where it should have gone and sank into the trunk of the tree behind it. Letting out a breath while figuring what he needed to do to compensate for his mistake, Clint eased the Colt back into its spot at his hip.

When he drew again, he was a little slower, but managed to cut the exact branch he'd intended to hit with a single, clean shot. He shifted his aim, fired again, and only missed by a fraction of an inch.

For any other marksman, the results would have been plenty good enough. For Clint, however, every fraction of an inch that he was off nagged at him like a burr that had made its way inside his boot. As he fired a few more rounds, Clint thought about some modifications he could make to his gun. If his wound had been more severe, he would have gotten to work on that very thing. But since he was already feeling a lot better now that the lead was out of his shoulder, Clint simply figured out the best way to make up the difference by adjusting his grip on the pistol as well as his timing when pulling the trigger. By the time he'd emptied another cylinder, Clint was satisfied with his results.

Nodding with quiet satisfaction, Clint reloaded the Colt and dropped it back into his holster. He took his time walking back so the cold air had a chance to seep all the way down to the marrow in his bones. Sometimes, there was something in the cold that made a man feel like he'd just been cleansed. Unlike the heat, which brought out sweat and bitter odors, the cold made everything seem pure.

The walk back to town wasn't as long as Clint would have liked. When he got back, he picked out a restaurant, went in, and had a big meal of pork chops, mashed potatoes, and fresh bread. When he stepped out of the restaurant, news was spreading about the trouble that had occurred at Rozekiel.

"Did you hear about what happened at that loony bin?" the clerk at Clint's hotel asked.

Just to get a feel for what was being said, Clint replied, "I'm not sure. What happened?"

"Seems a whole bunch of them crazy fellas busted out of there. The law rode up there and everything!"

"How bad was it?"

"I hear at least half a dozen of the boys who work at the place were killed and three or four of the loons got away."

Even though Clint knew better than to believe everything he heard through word of mouth, those figures seemed well within the realm of possibility. "How'd you come by that information?" he asked.

"One of the ladies who works there rents a room from me. She told me herself."

"What room is she in?" Clint asked. "I'd like to go up and check on her."

"That's real neighborly of you. She did seem awfully rattled. Give a knock on the door to room number twelve and send her my regards."

"I'll be sure to do that."

TEN

When Clint knocked on the door to room twelve, he didn't get an answer.

He knocked again and waited for a bit without getting so much as a peep from inside.

After he'd given up and turned his back on the room completely, he was surprised to hear a door open and someone step outside. Clint turned around to find a short redhead stepping out of room number twelve and easing the door shut behind her. Her hair was loose and hanging as if she'd been lying down a few seconds ago. The light red hair brought out the smooth paleness of her face and neck.

Once Clint saw where she'd come from, he stopped and walked back toward her room.

"Was that you knocking just now?" the redhead asked.

Clint nodded. "It sure was. I hope I wasn't disturbing you."

"Not at all," she said as she walked over to him. She was dressed in a simple, dark blue dress that was modestly cut in a bit at her waist and flowed down to her ankles. At the moment, she was barefoot. She didn't seem to mind that, however, and padded over to Clint without making a creak upon the floorboards.

"If this is a bad time, I could always come back later," Clint offered.

"Now's as good a time as any. What do you need?"

"Do you work at Rozekiel Sanitarium?"

"Yes," she replied with a nod. "Why do you ask?"

"You probably know there was some trouble there today. I was there as well. My name's Clint Adams, by the way."

The redhead smiled and offered her hand. "I know who you are. I was there and I saw what you did. You were very brave. My name is Sarah."

The moment Clint shook her hand, he noticed the strength in Sarah's grip. Even with that strength, she still felt smooth and soft in Clint's grasp. She rose on the balls of her feet as if allowing herself to be swept up in the simple movement of Clint's greeting. Sarah cocked her head to one side and smiled playfully once Clint released her.

"Was everything wrapped up at Rozekiel?" Clint asked.

"Oh, yes. It was a mess, but all the pieces got put back together." Glancing toward the lobby, she lowered her voice and added, "Maybe we shouldn't talk out in the hall like this. Folks in this town just love to spread scary stories about what goes on at Rozekiel."

"I'm sure they do. All I wanted to know was if everyone was all right and if—"

Sarah reached up to brush her fingers against Clint's lips. It was only a flutter of movement, but it was enough to stop Clint in midsentence. All the while, she kept a smirk on her face and rocked back and forth upon her feet. "Not out here," she whispered. "I'll get in trouble if I start up more rumors. The doctors really don't like that."

"Fine. Maybe I can catch up with you some other time."

"Now's a good time. This just isn't a good place. What room are you in?"

"I'm right over there," Clint said as he pointed to his

door. "But it's been a long day for everyone and I don't mind waiting for a while. Perhaps we can have lunch or dinner sometime?"

Sarah nodded, but eyed him as if he were a fresh cut of beef on her plate. Even after Clint turned and walked to his room, he could feel her watching him intently.

Turning around to glance back, Clint saw that she'd already walked to her own door and was pulling it open. The only sound she made was when the hinges gave a little creak before she stepped into her room. Sarah turned as if she could feel his gaze just as much as Clint could feel hers and gave him a little wave.

Clint remained outside his room to watch Sarah's door, even after she'd closed it behind her. Something about her struck him as peculiar. Then again, considering how he'd spent the rest of his day, Clint guessed his own definition of peculiar might have been skewed a bit. Shrugging, he went into his room and walked over to the water basin.

After tossing his hat onto the bed, Clint dipped his hands into the water and splashed some on his face. Before the water's chill could work its way through his entire face, Clint heard a knock on his door. He considered ignoring the knock in the hopes that whoever was outside would just keep walking.

Since the knocking only became more insistent, Clint dried off his face and answered the door.

"This is a much better place to talk," Sarah said as she walked past Clint and into his room.

ELEVEN

As she scooted past him, Sarah let her hand brush against the front of Clint's jeans. "I hope this is still a good time," she said.

"Sure, but . . ."

"But what?" Sarah asked as she locked her eyes on to his. Her hand was drifting once more below Clint's belt. For the time being, she seemed content to leave it there. "What you did at Rozekiel was more than just brave. You saved my life."

"Did I? I don't even recall you being there."

She nodded slowly and positioned herself so she was standing directly in front of him with her breasts pressed against Clint's chest. Raising herself up a bit on her tiptoes, she leaned against him even harder and told him, "I was there all right. You might not have seen me, but I sure saw you. If you hadn't gotten those men out of the kitchen, I would have been stabbed or . . . or worse."

"I don't know if there's a whole lot worse than that," Clint said.

"Well, after what you did, you deserve a whole lot better."

Before Clint could say another word, Sarah slid down along him and let her hands drift over Clint's chest and stomach. When she was on her knees, she ran her hands along his belt and worked to loosen his jeans. When Clint tried to unbuckle his gun belt, she placed her hand upon his and whispered, "Leave it."

She kept her fingertips on the spare bullets on the belt as she pulled his jeans down just enough to get her hand inside them. Clint was going to unbuckle his belt just to make her job easier, but was stopped when he felt her lips graze along his hardening cock. Sarah reached out to trace her finger along the Colt's handle as she took more of his growing erection into her mouth.

Clint let out a slow breath and removed his gun belt. "Don't want you to hurt yourself," he said.

Looking up at him with a pout, Sarah wrapped her hand all the way around him and stroked his penis while wrapping her lips around its tip. She continued stroking and then gradually sucked on him even harder until she could feel Clint reach around to slide one hand against the back of her head. She took his direction to heart and placed both of her hands on his hips so she could slide her mouth all the way down to the base of his shaft.

She sucked him in long, even motions. Her lips clenched tighter around him and her tongue rubbed along the bottom of his cock. When she had him completely in her mouth, she made a soft purring sound that curled Clint's toes within his boots.

Feeling Clint's hands take hold of her arms and pull her up, Sarah got to her feet and once more showed him the cute little pout. "Did I do something wrong?" she asked. "I just wanted to show my appreciation."

"That's just fine," Clint replied as he moved her over to his bed. "Now I want to show you something."

He stepped out of his pants while she pulled his shirt open. Clint then reached under her skirt so he could feel beneath her underwear and let his fingers wander through the downy hair between her legs. When he found one spot in particular, Sarah's knees weakened and she sat down on the bed.

Clint peeled her clothes off and crawled onto the bed as Sarah scooted back to accommodate him. Within seconds, she was lying on her back and opening her legs so Clint could settle between them.

"So," she asked with wide eyes and a very unconvincingly innocent expression on her face, "what do you want to show me?"

She was able to maintain her innocent act right up to the moment that Clint eased his rigid cock inside her and pushed it all the way in. Then she closed her eyes and leaned her head back while sighing. "Oh, now I see."

As Clint slowly pumped between her legs, he took in the sight of Sarah beneath him. Her skin was the color of milk and was just as smooth to the touch. Even her nipples were pale and almost blended in with the creamy surface of her rounded breasts. When he started pumping faster, Clint watched as Sarah eased her hands behind her head and arched her back to savor every last stroke.

Whenever he pulled back, he could feel Sarah's legs tighten around him as if she would never allow him to leave. That way, when he pushed forward again, he slammed into her even harder. Clint leaned forward a bit and placed both his hands upon her breasts. As he massaged her, he quickened his pace until he knew he was about to push Sarah over the edge.

Drawing closer and closer to her climax, Sarah began to pull in her breaths in short gasps. She turned her head to one side and pumped her own hips up and down to match Clint's rhythm. Soon, she propped herself up using both arms and wriggled so Clint hit just the right spot whenever he entered her. Once he'd found that spot, her orgasm wasn't long in coming.

Clint could feel her muscles tense and could hear the

little, pleasured moans coming from the back of Sarah's throat. When she felt the first hint of a climax, Sarah locked her eyes on to Clint and pumped her hips even faster. By now, Clint could feel a difference as well. Her wet little pussy tightened around his cock as Sarah's entire body trembled with a powerful climax.

She kept her upper body propped up, but leaned her head back so her red hair spilled over her shoulders and onto the pillow. Sarah opened her legs as wide as she could, allowing Clint to bury his cock deep inside her.

Just when it seemed she was going to let out a moan that would echo throughout the entire room, she swallowed it and clenched her lips shut in forced silence. Clint took that as a challenge and slipped one hand beneath her so he could lift her backside off the bed and pump into her from a new angle.

Sarah's eyes snapped open in an expression that made her surprise very obvious. She looked down to watch him enter her as if she didn't know what Clint might do next. She seemed surprised again when Clint knelt between her legs, ran his other hand down over the front of her body, and then rubbed the spot just above her pussy with his thumb.

Now it was a fight for Sarah to remain silent. She started to moan several times, but kept from making a sound. Finally, she lay back and pressed the back of one hand over her mouth and let out a muffled scream.

Clint would have liked to keep testing her, but was a bit too close to his own climax for that sort of game. He grabbed her hips in both hands and pumped into her with all the steam he'd built up so far. Sarah continued to writhe and only let out a prolonged groan when Clint exploded inside her. Even after he stopped moving, Clint could feel Sarah twitching her lower body until the last bit of pleasure worked its way through her system.

She lay on her back and eased her hand away from her mouth so she could nibble the side of one of her own fingers. Watching Clint move so he could drop onto the mattress beside her, she flipped onto her side and rubbed his chest.

"Thank you, Clint Adams," she whispered.

Clint chuckled. "Oh, no. Thank you."

Suddenly, Sarah sat up and hopped off the bed. By the time Clint caught sight of her again, she'd already collected her clothes and was slipping them on.

"Where are you going?" he asked when he saw her skip toward the door.

"Don't fret. I'm sure we'll see each other again."

"You don't have to leave just yet."

"Yes," she replied as she pulled open his door. "I think I do."

TWELVE

Clint took the next few minutes to collect himself and think about what had just happened with Sarah. He went back to the water basin and splashed some more water onto his face as his thoughts continued to flow through his mind. The longer they flowed, however, the less he liked them.

It had been a crazy day, but Clint had certainly had worse.

Sarah had done some peculiar things, but he'd seen a whole lot more peculiar than her.

Even so, there was something that just didn't set right with Clint. He couldn't quite put his finger on it, but something was just off.

Was it something that had been said, or perhaps something that hadn't been said?

Clint checked his holster to find the Colt was still right where it should be. With his hand still resting on the gun's grip, Clint remembered the look on Sarah's face when she'd touched the pistol. He was certain that she would have been perfectly happy if he'd left the gun on when they'd been in bed. In fact, Clint thought she might have preferred it that way.

Glancing quickly about the room, Clint felt his blood

pumping faster through his veins. Things were a little tousled here and there, but no more than could be expected after what had happened. And then Clint heard something. It wasn't too loud, but more of a sound that was just loud enough to be heard—a sound that could easily go unnoticed, but stood out as soon as Clint was able to pick it out.

Footsteps.

They weren't hurried boots thumping against the floor, but were a whole lot quieter than that. In fact, they were more like the quick padding of feet that were trying to go unnoticed and had almost pulled off the trick. They reminded Clint of Sarah's footsteps when she'd come into his room before being invited.

Clint had pulled on his boots and most of his clothes by the time he'd reached his door. He then opened the door a crack and took a look outside to find nobody in the hall. He snapped his eyes in the other direction to catch what could have been a hint of movement at the stairs that led down to the lobby. Pulling open the door as quietly as he could, Clint did his best to mimic those quiet footsteps as he headed to the stairs to get a look at the lower floor.

There was plenty of movement down those stairs, but that was only because several people were moving around in the lobby and heading toward the restaurant in the back of the building. Clint might have gone downstairs for a better look if he had been more than half dressed. That was about the time when he realized the only thing that had drawn him out of his room was a set of jangling nerves.

Suddenly, Clint felt like a fool for jumping at his own shadow. The fact of the matter was that he'd actually jumped at the *sound* of a shadow. It wasn't completely accurate, but was close enough to describe the faint hints of sound that he thought he'd heard.

The icing on the cake was when a well-dressed woman in the lobby looked up to find Clint standing at the top of the stairs. She placed one hand up to her neck and turned away as if she was afraid of why such a rough-looking man might be staring at her. Clint grinned uncomfortably and walked back toward his room.

Rather than open his own door, he walked all the way down to Sarah's door and knocked on it. There was no answer.

"Open up, Sarah. It's Clint." When he didn't get an answer he added, "Clint Adams."

Having already felt anxious and foolish in the space of a few minutes, Clint went right back to feeling anxious. He leaned toward the door and was unable to hear so much as the slightest bit of movement inside the room.

He knocked again. "Is anyone in there?"

This time, Clint did hear something. It was a voice that was a little too muffled to just be coming from inside the next room. More than that, the voice had a definite panicked edge to it.

"Hello?" he asked.

The voice was louder, but still muffled. The panic in that voice was strong enough to make Clint's heart skip a beat.

Hoping he wasn't about to make a very big mistake, Clint leaned his shoulder against the door and shoved. It creaked a bit, but didn't quite give. One more shove was all it took to get the door open. Clint's momentum caused him to stumble inside, where he found a woman tied to a chair with a gag stuffed into her mouth.

THIRTEEN

The first thing Clint noticed about the woman bound to the chair was that she wasn't Sarah. She watched him with wide, frightened eyes and reflexively squirmed as Clint rushed into the room. Once she got a closer look at him, she relaxed a bit.

"Hold still a second," Clint said as he took out his pocketknife. The blade sliced through the ropes without too much trouble, so Clint hunkered down to cut the ropes tying the woman's feet together at the ankles. As he freed her, Clint got a closer look at the woman.

She had a thin frame and long, straight blond hair. Once the gag was out of her mouth, Clint was able to get a full look at her face. "You were at Rozekiel," he said. "Weren't you one of Dr. Wolcott's helpers?"

Nodding while massaging the feeling back into her wrists, the blonde replied, "I am. My name's—"

"Heather!" Clint said as he snapped his fingers. "Now I remember. What are you doing here?"

Now that she was no longer bound to the chair, Heather couldn't get away from it fast enough. She knocked the chair over as she backed herself up against a wall. "I live here," she said. "I've been renting this room since I came to work for Dr. Wolcott."

"You rent this room?" Clint asked. He didn't even need to see her nod in response to that question for him to get a sinking feeling in the pit of his stomach. "Who tied you up? What happened here?"

Pointing toward the door, Heather said, "They might still be out there."

"Who?"

"A man and a woman! The woman had red hair and the man was one of Dr. Wolcott's patients. They just left."

Rather than leave the room again, Clint went to the window and looked outside. He didn't see anyone in the street, but he could hear the pounding of hooves moving away from the hotel. "Damn!" Clint grunted. Just as he was about to close the window, he spotted someone running across the street amid a flurry of skirts that she held bunched up around her waist. The red hair streaming behind her as she ran drew his attention even more.

"Stay here," Clint said as he climbed out the window.

Heather said something to him, but Clint was already outside and making too much noise while skidding along the hotel's front awning to hear her. Even as he was about to lose his balance and launch himself into a fall that would surely break his neck, Clint kept his focus on the commotion on the street below him.

Actually, the commotion was a little ways down the street near the corner. From what he could tell, someone was kicking up a whole lot of dirt as they tried to push their way through the crowd in the saloon district and still build up speed to tear farther down the street. Clint might have been able to see a little more, but his concentration was broken when he hit the edge of the hotel's awning.

The side of Clint's foot knocked against the awning and sent a jolt of pain up to his knee. He managed to correct himself before snapping his leg, but his momentum was still carrying him forward and into empty air. At the last second, Clint hopped up, twisted his body around, and then dropped over the side.

He stretched out both arms, but wasn't able to get a firm grip on the awning. Only the tips of one set of fingers caught the wooden edge, but that was enough to slow him up a bit before his boots hit the ground. Clint's entire body snapped like a whip as he hung from the awning and his shoulder screamed in pain. Less than a second later, he lost his grip and dropped the last few feet to street level.

After his boots touched solid ground, Clint paused for a second to see what bones he'd broken. Nothing hurt too badly, except his shoulder. He realized he had probably opened some stitches, but he wasn't bleeding so he started walking toward the noisy corner. After a few more steps, he knew he'd only bumped himself around during his fall so he broke into a full run.

There were plenty of folks along both sides of the street. The ones who weren't looking at the corner were gawking at Clint with wide eyes and had shock written across their faces. Fortunately, Clint's dramatic exit from the hotel gave him enough pull with that crowd to push them aside without needing to touch a single one of them. Those folks were willing to get the hell out of Clint's way as soon as he ran in their direction.

The commotion at the corner had died down a bit by the time Clint got there. In the space of those few seconds, the people milling about in front of the saloons were already closing the gaps that the previous runner had made. As Clint pushed through some of them, he saw the hindquarter of a horse galloping down the street and rounding another corner.

Turning to the first man he could find, Clint asked, "Who was on that horse?"

"There was two of 'em," the man replied. "Some red-headed lady and a fella."

Clint didn't stand still long enough to hear any more. He

bolted down the street and ducked into the first alley he could find that veered off in the same direction the horse had turned. The alley was dark and cluttered with everything from broken crates to stray cats. Clint dodged or jumped over everything he could and managed to emerge at the other end of the alley in full stride.

He paused for a second to get his bearings. In that time, he heard the rumble of horses' hooves to his right. Clint turned and started running again before he could tell that someone else was walking in that direction. Although Clint managed to turn his body sideways, he still knocked some drunk aside in his haste to get to those horses.

A quick look over his shoulder told Clint that the drunk was all right. From there, Clint ran as fast as his legs would carry him until he caught sight of the horses that were racing for the edge of town. Just as the other man in front of the saloon had told him, there were two horses. Clint couldn't quite make out who was in the saddle before they split apart and ran in opposite directions.

Swearing under his breath, Clint adjusted his course so he could try and cut off the horse that was headed toward him. He circled around a small dry goods store on the corner and reemerged in the street just as Sarah rode her horse past him. Her red hair caught Clint's attention like a flag that had been waved in front of his face and he followed that flag with an extra dose of steam in his stride.

Clint wasn't sure if she'd seen him or not. Sarah rode toward the next corner and had to pull back on her reins to avoid colliding with a cart being pulled by two startled mules. Hoping that she was going to try to meet up with the other rider, Clint ran across the street and raced down the boardwalk less than twenty yards behind Sarah's horse. She was just now snapping her reins again, but Clint ducked into an alley to his right and made the first left he could when he came out of it. His gamble paid off, since he was able to cross the next street just as Sarah had rounded the corner to come straight at him.

Judging by the look on her face, she hadn't realized that Clint was chasing after her all this time. That surprised expression only grew when Clint launched off both feet to fly at her with his arms outstretched.

Sarah's instinct was to simply lean back and try to protect herself by raising her arms. This actually helped cushion the blow once Clint's arms wrapped around her midsection and pulled her from her saddle. Since the horse was moving forward and Sarah was now moving backward, her feet came free of the stirrups, and the reins were neatly plucked from her hands.

Her legs were flailing as she dropped, but stopped when she hit the ground. Clint had been able to tighten his grip around her, so he turned them both in midair before they hit the ground. Both of their sides pounded against the street, but Clint turned himself to absorb most of the impact. Thankfully, he kept his wounded shoulder from taking the brunt of the fall.

For a few seconds, both of them just lay there.

Sarah blinked her eyes in a flutter of lashes as she slowly regained her senses. She was rumpled, and most of the wind had been knocked out of her, but she was healthy enough to scramble to her feet in a matter of seconds. Clint almost lost his hold on her, but snagged a handful of her dress before she could get away.

"Oh, no you don't!" he said as he pulled her closer.

Even though her feet were barely touching the ground, Sarah continued to kick and flail as if she were running away. She swung her fists back at Clint, but lost some of her steam when she saw her horse continue running down the street without her.

FOURTEEN

Clint didn't allow Sarah's feet to rest upon the ground until he felt her go limp in his arms. "Thought you'd get away from me, did you?" he asked.

She looked over her shoulder at him and grinned. "I thought I'd tired you out pretty good," she said in the same breathless tone she'd had when moaning in his room not too long ago. "Maybe I'll ride you harder next time."

"I don't think there's going to be a next time."

"Yeah," she said as she looked around and narrowed her eyes. "You might just be right about that."

Clint took a look around as well, but not because of anything Sarah had done or said. He was more concerned about all the people on either side of the street, as well as the few horses and riders in the street itself. Those people were all gaping at Clint and Sarah, but were now closing in with some bad intentions reflected in their eyes.

For the most part, those scowls were directed at Clint.

One of the men on the boardwalk stepped forward as his hand drifted toward the gun at his hip. "What in the hell do you think you're doin' to that lady?"

Still holding Sarah up so she couldn't gain any traction, Clint replied, "This isn't your affair, mister."

"The hell it isn't. I saw you run up and attack that lady!"

"Me too!" another bystander added. "He knocked her clean off'a her horse! He could'a killed her."

"Maybe he was tryin' to kill her," the first one said. "Is that it? Were you tryin' to kill that lady, mister?"

Clint looked around at the people who were closing in on him. Although plenty of those people were inching their hands toward guns or even gripping brooms as if they meant to swing them at Clint's head, Clint refrained from doing anything to egg them on. Of course, that was easier said than done.

And then, with timing that couldn't have been any better, Sarah let her body droop forward and pushed out a wrenching sob. "I can't get away from him," she cried. "Oh, Lord, why won't he just leave me alone?"

Clint backed toward the closest wall and dragged Sarah along with him. He gritted his teeth as the men surrounding him responded to Sarah's act. A few of them were gathering the courage needed to draw their guns. If he allowed things to get that far, Clint knew they would only get worse.

Just then, another voice made itself known. It wasn't one of the voices from the men in the crowd and it didn't come from Clint or Sarah. It was the voice of someone who obviously wasn't accustomed to shouting, but was worked up enough to be heard above all others.

"That's no lady!" Heather shouted.

A few of the nearby men turned toward the sound of her voice. More important, some of those men recognized her.

"You know her, Heather?" the first angry man asked.

Heather stepped forward and nodded. "She escaped from Rozekiel earlier this evening and almost killed me so she could get away."

The very mention of the sanitarium caused all of the locals to bristle.

"What about him?" the second angry man asked as he slapped his hand against the grip of his pistol.

Heather stepped forward enough to place a hand on the second man's shoulder. "He saved my life," she said. "And he chased this woman down so she can go back to Rozekiel where she belongs. And," she added with a tired smile, "he was a lot gentler than I would have been in doing so."

Slowly, the men began to nod and ease their hands away from their guns. Sarah had managed to push out some tears by now, but that wasn't enough to sway anyone back to her side. Once she realized that much, she spat a few obscenities and tried to kick her way free from Clint's grasp.

"We heard the law had to ride out to that loony bin," the first man said. "You need some help with that one?"

For a second, Clint was thrown off by the sudden shift of hostility. Now that he was certain the crowd was on his side and looking at Sarah as if she were a pariah, Clint replied, "I don't suppose any of you saw where the other one went?"

After a few confused looks among members of the crowd, the first man asked, "There was another one?"

Sarah looked at Clint with a self-satisfied grin.

He grabbed her by the back of her collar and held her so she was forced to walk a few steps in front of him. "Don't look so happy," Clint told her. "You're not out of this yet."

FIFTEEN

Heather was bursting at the seams to talk to him, but Clint had her keep quiet as best she could until all three of them got back to her room. Once inside, Clint sat Sarah down in the same chair where Heather had been tied. He then salvaged as much rope as he could and made up for the pieces that had been cut by shredding a few of the bedsheets. By the time they were done, Sarah was bound up so tightly that she could barely squirm.

Heather tried to talk again, but Clint stopped her with an upraised finger and then pointed that same finger to the pillows. She handed one over, but was obviously confused as to why he would need it. After Clint stripped the pillow of its case and then wrapped the case around Sarah's head, the confusion on Heather's face turned to an amused grin.

"There now," Clint said after he'd covered Sarah's eyes as well as her ears with the pillow case. "I feel a little safer talking around her now."

Holding up a hand as a signal to Heather, Clint spoke in a voice that was just above a whisper. "Nod if those ropes are too tight, Sarah."

Although he wasn't expecting a gentle nod, Clint knew that she would have responded in some way. Since she didn't even twitch toward the sound of his voice, Clint knew that she must not have heard him. Even so, he walked to the opposite side of the room with Heather beside him.

"So tell me what happened here," Clint said.

Heather glanced over at Sarah, only to find the other woman straining against her bonds and moving her head in various directions that had nothing to do with where Clint had gone. Speaking in a voice that was a little lower than Clint's, Heather replied, "I was sent home after what happened at Rozekiel. I barely got into my room before someone knocked on my door. When I opened it, someone hit me."

When Heather spoke, she motioned toward her right temple. That's when Clint saw the blood encrusted on her scalp that had been mostly covered by her hair. Gently lifting her hair to get a look at the wound, Clint asked, "Who hit you?"

"I don't know, but when I opened my eyes again, I was tied to that chair."

"You said there were two of them. Do you know who the other was?"

She nodded. "He was another patient at Rozekiel. I recognized him because Dr. Wolcott worked with him a lot. His name is Solomon Reyes."

"Did you hear them talking? Anything they might have said could be useful."

After thinking it over for a few seconds, she shrugged and said, "A lot of it seems jumbled since my head hurt so much. All I could hear for a while was ringing in my ears. That redhead was close to me for a while. She said she saw a gunfighter in this hotel and that she recognized him from the fight at Rozekiel. I guess she meant you."

"Yeah. Probably."

"She left and said she was going to keep you busy for a while and that she would kill you if she needed to. I'm so glad she didn't kill you. Did she try to hurt you?"

Thinking back to what Sarah had done to keep him busy, Clint couldn't help but feel a little uneasy. He was ashamed at first, but knew there was no way for him to recognize a patient from the sanitarium on sight. Still, being strung along the way he had didn't set well with him at all.

"It sounds like she was just supposed to keep me distracted," Clint said. "I wish I had known who she was at the time."

"How could you know?" Heather asked without hesitation.

"Actually, I thought she was you." Seeing the confusion on Heather's face, Clint added, "I was told the person renting this room worked at the sanitarium. When I came to the door, Sarah answered and . . . well . . . she was convincing enough to do the trick."

"That was you who knocked?"

"Yeah. I didn't know you were in here tied up at the time. I feel so bad about leaving you here."

"You're the one who got me out," Heather said. "You're also the one who tore after those two and managed to haul one all the way back. That's more than enough to clear the slate with me. In fact, I think I owe you."

"And you're the one who came after me to speak on my behalf with those locals. You don't owe me a thing."

Although she showed Clint a warm smile, Heather's eyes were drawn back to Sarah. "What do we do with her?"

"Hopefully, we can get her to tell us where to find Solomon Reyes. I don't like the thought of one of those escaped killers riding around free as a bird."

"You think she'll tell you anything?"

"Not at first," Clint admitted. "But I've got a few ideas on how to loosen her tongue a bit."

SIXTEEN

After discussing a few more things with Heather, Clint walked over to where Sarah was sitting. Neither he nor Heather said anything to each other as he paced back and forth in front of Sarah's chair. He then circled the chair a few more times and paced behind it until Sarah couldn't help but respond to the noises he was making. Sarah didn't say anything, but she did look around and cock her head as if to try to pick up whatever noises she could.

Clint waited until Sarah was truly paying attention before he walked over to Heather and spoke to her in a voice that was just loud enough to be heard through the material wrapped around Sarah's ears. The words Clint said didn't matter. All he cared about was that Sarah was listening and straining to hear more.

Finally, Heather spoke up. "Dr. Wolcott will not like that. He'll want to get her back into Rozekiel as soon as possible."

"I don't care what the doctor wants," Clint replied. "This woman hurt you and she meant to kill me. I'll see she hangs for it!" With that, he stomped over to Sarah, grabbed the makeshift blindfold, and yanked it off her head.

Sarah shook the red hair from her eyes and blinked

furiously. Before she could get her bearings, her entire
field of vision was filled by Clint's angry face.

"Where's your partner?" he snarled.

"Why would I tell you?" Sarah replied petulantly.

"To save your own neck. I've been told you set out to
kill me," Clint replied. "Is that true?"

Glancing toward Heather, Sarah shrugged and then
looked at Clint with wide eyes. "I didn't try to kill you,
Clint. The way I remember, you had a real good time when
I came to your room. Are you going to hang me for that?"

"What about those people who were killed back at that
sanitarium? I suppose you didn't have anything to do with
that."

"I didn't!" Sarah snapped.

"So you just happened to tag along when the real killers
escaped?"

"Yes. That's what happened."

"Bullshit," Clint barked. "Innocent people don't run
away in the company of murderers and they sure as hell
don't tie women to chairs and threaten their lives."

"I don't know," Sarah said as she wriggled beneath the
ropes tying her ankles and wrists together. "This isn't so
bad. I wouldn't even mind if you decided to have a little
more fun with me."

Clint looked at her for a few seconds and then shook his
head. Wrapping the blindfold around her head again, he
grumbled, "I'm through with you. Since there's a price being offered for the capture of anyone who escaped from
Rozekiel, I'd say that means I get to have my cake and eat
it too."

"Where are you taking her?" Heather asked.

"I'm going to have a word with the ones putting up that
reward money. I need to check to see if the offer's the same
whether they're brought in dead or alive."

"What reward?" Sarah asked. "There's no reward!"

Pausing to watch Sarah quietly for a second, Clint was able to pick up on just enough panic in her movements to know she was taking the bait. He stomped toward the door while saying, "And I may even get something from the law when I tell them she was one of the patients who killed some of those workers."

"I didn't kill anyone!" Sarah said. "You can't prove any of that!"

"I won't need to prove a damn thing." Clint pulled open the door, took a few more stomping steps, and then slammed it shut. Leaning against the door frame with his arms crossed, Clint watched Sarah carefully. He was even more careful to stay perfectly quiet and not move a muscle.

When he saw Heather start to approach Sarah, Clint raised a single finger to his lips and shook his head. Heather nodded slowly and stood her ground.

The longer she sat there in the quiet room, the more anxious Sarah got. Soon, she was twitching at every rattle of the window or bit of dirt that was blown against the outside wall. When someone actually did walk down the hall, Sarah looked in that direction and froze as if she was trying to absorb everything she could through the blindfold.

Finally, Clint removed the finger he'd placed against his lips and nodded. Heather took her cue and walked across the room in front of Sarah's chair.

Snapping her head to that movement, Sarah asked, "Who's that? I heard you! I know you're there!"

"It's only me," Heather replied. "You know . . . the one you tied up after your friend knocked me out?"

"Oh," Sarah replied with a hint of a grin. "I remember you. Is Clint really angry at me?"

"Why shouldn't he be? I told him about how you and your friend Solomon were going to kill him."

"You didn't hear everything. You certainly didn't hear what Clint and I did when we were alone."

"I don't care about that," Heather replied. "You lied to him. You and Solomon hurt me and you hurt plenty of good people a lot worse. You killed plenty of them as well."

"That wasn't me. That was Solomon's doing. His hands were covered in blood. Not mine."

"You're the one that's here, so you've got to answer for what you've done."

"Is Clint really going to hand me over for some reward?" Sarah asked.

Glancing reflexively over to where Clint was standing, Heather replied, "I suppose so."

"You work at the sanitarium. You work with the doctor. Won't he want to get us all back so we can get well?"

"I'm sure he would."

Putting a sly tone in her voice, Sarah said, "I'm sure you'd be the one to be rewarded if you brought me back there. Clint's just after money, but you and Dr. Wolcott are healers."

Clint could tell that got under Heather's skin a bit. Even though he'd warned her about what Sarah might say to get out, he knew that some nerves still hurt when they were hit. Still, Heather was doing a good job of following what little directions he'd given her before starting in on this line of questioning.

"Good men were killed," Heather said. "They were healers, too. It won't matter what I try to do. The law will want to make someone pay for those killings."

"Someone should pay, but you wouldn't just throw anyone to the wolves, would you?"

"What other choice do I have?"

Gritting her teeth, Sarah squirmed some more and mulled that over. To stoke the fire under her a bit, Clint rattled the door handle as if someone were trying to get in.

"Solomon's headed north," Sarah blurted out. "If I help you find him, I want you to swear I go back to Rozekiel and not to jail. I ain't about to hang for what he did!"

Clint smiled like a cat with a mouthful of canary.

SEVENTEEN

After knocking on the door and opening it for himself, Clint pretended to come back into the room so Heather could explain things to him. Sarah flinched back and forth between the sounds of their voices, being sure to add her own two cents whenever she saw fit. Even though the entire conversation was for show, Clint heard enough from Sarah to know that the redhead had bought into the line she'd been fed.

Doing a good job of pretending to be the devil's advocate, Heather pleaded, "There's been enough bloodshed already. Let's just take her back to Rozekiel where she belongs."

"To hell with that," Clint growled.

"I'll go quietly!" Sarah begged. "I'll tell you whatever you need and then I'll do whatever you want. I won't cause any trouble."

The most encouraging part of that for Clint was the fact that Sarah hadn't tried to get under Clint's skin or make any advances toward him just then. So far, it was the first time he'd seen the redhead without her acting as if she had him wrapped around her little finger. "You won't cause any trouble? And I suppose you'll also just tell me where to ride so I can be miles away before I know you lied to me?"

Her twitch was gone as quickly as it had showed up. It was enough to convince any cardplayer that they'd hit a nerve. "He rode off and left me behind! That bastard didn't even try to come back for me! Why should I care what happens to him from here on?"

"We'll just see about that," Clint replied. He stomped back toward the door and motioned for Heather to come closer. Dropping his voice to a whisper, he asked, "Can you keep an eye on her if I leave for a bit?"

"I suppose," Heather replied, even though she was obviously scared.

"On second thought . . ." Clint walked back to Sarah and double-checked all the knots tying her to the chair. He even tightened as many as he could before dragging the chair to a corner and facing her toward a wall. On his way back to the door, he took hold of Heather's arm so she would come along with him.

Once they were in the hall, Clint shut the door. "She's not going anywhere," he said. "If she could get out of those knots, I wouldn't want you in that room with her anyway. I'm in that room right down the hall."

"Where are you going?" Heather asked.

"I want to check back at Rozekiel and see how everything wound up. Is there anything else you can tell me?"

After thinking for a moment, Heather shook her head. "I was sent away when things were still a mess. I know at least half a dozen workers were killed and more were hurt."

"How many escaped?"

"I don't know for sure. It's got to be more than just those two who came for me."

"Any idea why they came for you?" Clint asked.

"I think they just followed me from Rozekiel and wanted a place to hide for a bit."

Clint nodded and escorted Heather to his room. "You

stay put, but try to keep an eye on the door to your room. If you see it so much as budge, I want you to get help. If you hear anything fall or break in there, don't go in. Just get help. Understand?"

She nodded. "Maybe I should get help right now."

"Not just yet. I know we can't trust that woman, but I think we can use her to track down Solomon Reyes. You did real good back there, but it'll take more than that for us to get everything we need. I'd say the law's got their hands full right now, so the most I can do is help track down whoever I can. I'm going to need to bring Sarah along for a while to do that."

"I don't think the law would have a problem with that," Heather said. "They barely consider any of the patients at Rozekiel to be people."

"Maybe, but I doubt the doctors there would take kindly to loaning out their patients, even if it is for a good cause."

She closed her eyes for a moment and then nodded. "I want to come along."

"You just stay here and watch the door in case—"

"No," Heather interrupted. "If you ride out after Solomon, I want to come along. I've worked with Dr. Wolcott for long enough to know how to care for people with sicknesses like Solomon's and that woman's in there."

Clint was already shaking his head before she finished her sentence. "People have died. These two are dangerous and they'll be even more dangerous when we track them down."

"Do you truly know what you're dealing with?"

"Yes," Clint replied sternly. "Sick or not, a killer is a killer. I've dealt with plenty of them."

"So you truly are going to gun them down and drag their bodies back?"

"Not if I can help it."

"Good. Then since you know so much about patients

like Sarah and Solomon, I suppose you'll know exactly how to handle them if they have difficulties or behave oddly due to their conditions?"

Sighing, Clint replied, "I'll think of something."

"And if they happen to join up with more of the escaped patients," Heather continued, "I suppose you'll be able to recognize who they are, what's wrong with them, and whether or not they're dangerous?"

This time, Clint felt truly stuck. As if his long pause or the expression on his face didn't already give him away, he admitted, "I wouldn't be able to recognize all that right away, but—"

"But you would know them based on what Sarah told you?" Heather asked. "Or maybe you'd make your decisions like the workers who were tricked and killed during that escape?"

"Fine. Point taken. You can come, but you'll do as I say when it comes to laying low and you won't question me if things get rough."

Heather nodded. "It's a deal."

"This could be dangerous, you know."

"My job's always been a little dangerous, but I took it. Whoever else is out there didn't sign on to deal with the likes of these patients. I wanted to be a nurse to help people. With those patients out there, people need my help more than ever."

Clint patted her shoulder and watched as Heather walked to his room. For a woman who didn't carry a weapon, she was brave enough to walk into the fire. Now he had to keep her from getting burned.

EIGHTEEN

Clint wanted to have a word with Dr. Wolcott as well as the local law. Fortunately, when he rode back to Rozekiel Sanitarium, he was able to kill both birds with one stone. The sanitarium was still a mess, but it was more of a comfort to see so many armed men patrolling the grounds. More than a few of those men were also wearing badges.

One of the three men who spotted Clint riding up to the main building was a lawman. Although the lawman looked a bit nervous, he approached Clint with a shotgun nestled in the crook of his arm.

"Not any farther," the young man with the badge announced. "What are you doing here?"

"I'm Clint Adams. I was here during the escape."

Before the lawman could ask another question, Dr. Liam rushed down the path. "Let him pass, Deputy. Clint was a big help to us."

The deputy studied Clint through narrowed eyes, but moved his horse aside to let Clint go by. The other men with the deputy followed suit.

"I apologize for that, Mr. Adams," Dr. Liam said. "The marshal and his men have been understandably jumpy after . . . well . . . after what happened."

"Not a problem, Doctor," Clint said as he dismounted. "Although it would have been nice to see this sort of attention to detail before the patients started killing your workers."

Clint was a bit surprised at the barbed comment that had come out of him and, judging by the look on Dr. Liam's face, he was as well. Even so, the doctor shook it off pretty well.

"I suppose you're right about that," Dr. Liam said. "What can I do for you?"

"I just came by to see how everything turned out. Did you get a final tally on who got away?"

Dr. Liam winced again, but this time it seemed more because of what he wanted to say. "So far, it looks like we're missing five patients." Lowering his voice, he added, "That's not including the ones that were killed after the shooting started."

"I've already caught hell about that," someone groused from a few paces away. "But what the hell did you expect me to do once those loons were out and running wherever they pleased?"

Both Clint and Dr. Liam shifted their attention toward the source of those last words. They found a short man who looked to be somewhere in his sixties. The fellow had silver whiskers sprouting from his chin that looked just coarse and short enough to scrub the rust off an old anchor. His mustache completely covered his upper lip and did a passable job of obscuring the lower one as well. A narrow face and squinting eyes added even more of an edge to the harsh tone in his voice.

"Marshal Laherty," Dr. Liam said quickly, "this is Clint Adams. Clint, meet Marshal Laherty."

Although Clint extended his hand immediately, the marshal looked down at it first before shaking it. It seemed the lawman was concerned he might catch something, but he grudgingly shook Clint's hand anyway.

"So you're the man who started the shooting?" Laherty grunted.

Clint felt an annoyed twitch in his eye, but did his best to keep that sentiment from creeping into his voice when he replied, "I stepped in to rein in some of the patients before they could hurt anyone else, if that's what you mean."

"No, I mean you started the shooting. From what I was told, things hadn't gotten as far as shots being fired until you pulled your trigger. It was in the kitchen, right?"

"Yes. Some cooks were being held by patients with—"

"With knives," Laherty snapped. "Then you had to get trigger happy and all hell broke loose. If I had more room in my jail right now, I'd toss you in just for making my job harder."

"All due respect, Marshal," Clint said evenly, "but I would have thought your job was to handle the situation yourself instead of just cleaning up afterward."

Gritting his teeth as if he were actually choking on his own words, Marshal Laherty propped his hands on his hips and took another step closer to Clint. Apparently, his deputies recognized the marshal's growing anger because a few of them closed ranks around the older man.

"The last thing I need around here is a gunfighter," Laherty snarled. "You *comprendé*?"

Clint nodded, but kept quiet. He knew anything he said at that moment wouldn't exactly put him in the good graces of the law.

"You've already done enough, Adams," the marshal continued. "Now, get on your horse and let me and my boys do the rest."

Turning his back to Rozekiel Sanitarium, Clint waved a quick hand toward the lawmen and said, "Fine with me."

NINETEEN

Clint was almost back to the spot where Eclipse was waiting when Dr. Liam rushed over to him. The doctor was almost out of breath by the time he skidded to a stop and frantically tapped Clint on the shoulder.

"What is it, Doctor?" Clint asked.

"You'll have to . . . You really should . . ." Between the doctor's haggard breathing and the worried glances he kept throwing toward Marshal Laherty and the deputies, it was a toss-up as to whether Dr. Liam would snap his own neck or simply pass out from exhaustion. Dropping his voice to a wheezing whisper, he said, "You shouldn't take Marshal Laherty's words to heart. He's just upset because he was proven wrong."

"You'll have to be more specific. He strikes me as a man who's been wrong about a whole lot of things."

When Dr. Liam chuckled, it seemed to catch in his throat even more than the last few breaths he'd tried to take. "Dr. Wolcott and I have been begging him to put a deputy here, but the marshal has always refused. After tonight, it seems even his own men are questioning him."

Clint kept one hand on Eclipse's neck as he turned to face the doctor. "Maybe they should question him. I came here to see if I could help and I got slapped down before I could make the offer."

"I'm sure you have only the best intentions, but I wouldn't want you to put yourself at risk again to clean up this debacle. After all, this is the responsibility of the doctors here and now the law."

Even though the marshal's words still stuck in his craw, Clint had to admire Dr. Liam's effort to own up to what had happened. Acknowledging the doctor's effort with a nod, Clint asked, "What can I do to help? I'm here, so I might as well chip in."

"There's really nothing. The patients who got away . . . Well . . . I couldn't tell you where to begin in finding them. That's what we're trying to figure out now."

Clint looked around at the men crowding around the front of Rozekiel's main entrance. After dismissing Clint, Marshal Laherty was now doing his best to corral everyone else as he continued to bark orders and shove workers around. "Where's Dr. Wolcott?" Clint asked.

"Assessing the damage."

Now that he took a closer look at Dr. Liam's face, Clint could tell there was something nagging at the doctor like a tick skittering just under his collar. "What else did you want to say, Doctor?" Clint asked.

Although Dr. Liam struggled against spitting out what he wanted to say, he pushed himself until he did so. The doctor's nervousness, combined with his predicament, made it tough to say whether he was fighting to speak or to keep quiet. Whatever that struggle might have been, Dr. Liam said, "I feel horrible about what happened and I'm sure Dr. Wolcott feels the same. We knew these men were dangerous and we did our best to cure them, but things went bad and people got hurt."

"You don't have to tell me," Clint replied.

"We lost some good workers and even two doctors who

only wanted to help ease these people's troubled minds. Asking someone else to take the chance of getting hurt . . . asking someone like you to do that . . . well, it would be wrong. But allowing those patients to get away without doing everything possible to bring them back is wrong too. You're a good man, Clint, and I hate to ask you to do such a thing but . . ."

Clint reached out to place a hand upon Dr. Liam's shoulder. The doctor's muscles tensed like a coiled spring around the nervous fellow's neck. "You don't have to be afraid to ask, Doctor. It's the lesser of your two evils."

"Exactly," Dr. Liam said as he let out the breath he'd been holding. "And since you were going to offer your services anyway, you should know that they would be very much appreciated. The only thing is that I don't know how much help the marshal is going to be."

"I've already spoken to the marshal enough to know that I don't need his help. I could use a bit of help from you, though. In fact, that's the main reason I came all the way out here."

Dr. Liam's eyes widened as he nodded enthusiastically. "Anything I can do, Mr. Adams."

"First off, just call me Clint."

"Done."

"Second," Clint said, "you can tell me anything I might need to know about Solomon Reyes."

That name obviously struck a chord with Dr. Liam. "Solomon is one of the men who got away. Do you know where he might have gone?"

"Not exactly, but I think I've got a good way to track him down. Is there anything I should know if I do find him?"

"Solomon's afraid of enclosed spaces. He broke the arm of one of our workers after he was cooped up in a holding room for a few hours. He was just waiting for one of his treatments and when the worker came for him, Solomon was very violent."

"All right. Anything else?"

Dr. Liam thought for a few seconds and added, "He also doesn't do well on his own. Solomon tends to get confused when he's left to his own devices. He may even become catatonic. That means he may curl up and decide not to move. He may be unable to move."

Clint nodded and let the doctor finish what he was saying. Even though he had a good notion of what Dr. Liam was talking about, he wasn't offended by the doctor's tacked-on explanation. Dr. Liam didn't give the first hint that he was talking down to Clint in any way.

"What about a woman named Sarah?" Clint asked. "She's from here as well and has red hair."

"Do you think she's with Solomon?"

"Yes."

"Then that would be Sarah Davies," Liam explained. "She is the only woman who goes anywhere near Solomon, but that's just because we normally keep them apart. But I should warn you about her."

Just hearing that caused Clint to come up with a whole lot of guesses as to what Dr. Liam might say next. He wasn't quite expecting the words that followed.

"Sarah Davies must be returned to us intact and alive," Dr. Liam said. "I'm not trying to disparage you or your, um, methods, but getting her back is vital and she won't do us any good if she's harmed or dead. In fact, if she is harmed in any way, it could prove quite disastrous."

"That's an awfully harsh word, Doctor."

"And I don't use it lightly, I assure you. Do you know where she is?"

Although Clint only paused for a second, he did a lot of thinking in that short amount of time. In the blink of an eye, he weighed the pros and cons of telling Dr. Liam the truth in its entirety. He also thought about the job ahead and what could be gained or lost if Dr. Liam spread what he was told among everyone else at Rozekiel. If not for the doubts he had regarding Marshal Laherty, Clint's decision would have been a whole lot easier.

"She's one of the patients I might be able to track down," Clint said.

"If you find her, don't leave her alone with Solomon. Just bring her back as soon as you can!"

"That was my plan, Doctor."

TWENTY

Clint returned to his hotel and went straight up to Heather's room. He still had the key in his pocket, but he tested the door just to make sure he needed it. Thankfully, the door was still locked. After fitting in the key and turning it, he opened the door just enough to get a look inside.

He didn't hear anything in the room, so Clint took a few steps through the doorway. Keeping his hand upon the grip of his pistol, Clint kept walking until he saw the dark shape in the far corner. A few seconds later, he heard the sound of slow, steady breathing. Now that Clint's eyes were adjusted to the darkness, he could just make out the hint of red hair in the dim light filtering into the room. Also, Sarah's figure was easy to spot since her back was flush against the chair and her arms were tied behind her.

Clint left the room and locked the door behind him. He then went to his own room and knocked on the door before unlocking it. Spotting Heather as she snapped her head up and reflexively twitched at the sound of footsteps, he said, "It's just me, Heather."

As soon as she saw his face, Heather relaxed a bit. "Oh," she said as she placed a hand over her heart. "Clint. You startled me."

"Hope I didn't interrupt anything."

"Oh, no. Nothing like that. I've just been listening for every little sound and watching for any movement. I guess I wound myself up pretty tightly."

Clint stepped inside and shut the door. "Better safe than sorry. I had a word with Dr. Liam." A sour expression drifted onto his face as he added, "Had a few words with Marshal Laherty, as well."

A similar expression came onto Heather's face when she heard that. "Don't pay the marshal any mind. He's always like that."

Even though he could still feel the unpleasantness at mentioning Laherty's name, Clint had to grin at Heather's reaction. "At least I know he wasn't just an ass to me. Anyway, I suppose it's no surprise to you that we'd get a lot more done without the law."

"Are you sure about that? I mean, the marshal and his deputies aren't pleasant, but they're still the law."

"They've also got plenty to keep them busy right now. There are other patients running around who need to be tracked down. We're doing them a favor by going after these two."

"And we've already got one all wrapped up," Heather said.

"We sure do." Clint did his best to share Heather's enthusiasm, but he couldn't do it for long. "From what Dr. Liam told me, this Solomon fellow might be a handful. He talked about him as if he were some sort of a plague on his fellow man."

Heather nodded slowly. "We try not to treat patients like prisoners or like they're evil. It's part of the new approach to dealing with that kind of sickness."

"That sounds like you're reciting from a manual," Clint said.

Shrugging, she replied, "I am. Every so often, the doctors

get together and decide on what they should do with these people, and this is the newest line of thought."

"What do you think?"

"Well, I'm no doctor," she replied carefully. "But I've dealt with Solomon Reyes enough to know that he's a troubled man who is capable of hurting folks. He can't be allowed to be out there among regular people. I mean . . . people who aren't sick. I mean, sick like—"

"I know what you mean," Clint said as he gently stopped her before she continued to cover her tracks. "Solomon's not right in the head."

"More or less, but there's worse men in Rozekiel than him."

"The greater evil," Clint said. When he saw the questioning look on Heather's face, he added, "It's something Dr. Liam mentioned. Kind of like choosing the lesser of two evils."

"Oh, I see. If you're referring to the two patients we're after, I'd say Solomon is a greater evil than Sarah. I just hope that some of those other patients in Rozekiel didn't make it out of the sanitarium. And if they did, I pray Marshal Laherty can track them down."

Clint rubbed Heather's shoulders and found himself wrapping his arms around her. She was hesitant at first, but soon melted into his embrace and rested her cheek against him. After a few seconds of Clint doing nothing more than holding her, she relaxed a bit more.

"Let's just worry about one evil at a time," Clint said. "Speaking of which, I need to check on the little devil we've got tied up in the next room."

TWENTY-ONE

Clint made a few necessary arrangements and then headed out of town as soon as he was able. That allowed him and Heather to rest up for a bit and it also allowed them to get something to fill their stomachs. One of the arrangements Clint made was to buy a small cart from one of the locals. The next morning, he loaded the cart up with the one piece of cargo that needed to be moved. Unfortunately, the cargo wasn't too happy about the trip.

"What is the meaning of this?" Sarah asked when Clint finally relented and pulled down the material wrapped over her mouth.

"This is a cart," Clint replied as he looked at the small rickety collection of lumber that was hitched to Heather's horse. "I thought I removed your blindfold a while ago."

"To hell with the blindfold and to hell with you," Sarah hissed. "Why can't I ride on horseback like anyone else?"

"Because you're not anyone else. You're a wanted fugitive and a dangerous one if I'm to believe everything the law's been saying."

"The law doesn't know a damn thing about me." Slowly, the defiant scowl on Sarah's face melted away. "Do they?"

"I know we had our own deal," Clint replied. "If you don't want to be handed over as a murderer, you'll take me to Solomon Reyes."

Sarah shifted her mouth into a seductive pout to match the pleading tone in her voice. "I will, Clint. I just want to ride with you."

"I got this cart just for you and now you don't want it?"

"You can trust me. Honest."

Clint stared at her until his expression became harsher and more critical of what he'd just heard.

Since Sarah abandoned her baby doll act, it seemed she wasn't too surprised that Clint wasn't buying it. "All I have to do is let out a scream and these folks will all know you're hauling a woman around like a load of manure."

Nodding as he looked up and down the small road that led from the stable where he'd hitched up the cart and saddled Eclipse, Clint took a step back from Sarah and opened his arms as if to encompass the entire town. "You want to let everyone know you're here? Fine. It'll make it a little harder for me to find Solomon, but at least I can hand you over to Marshal Laherty right away. That would definitely save me some trouble."

Sarah didn't even bother looking around at the locals who were walking up and down the nearby street. She narrowed her eyes as if she were trying to burn through Clint's head and grumbled, "You're a horse's ass, Clint Adams."

"You ready to get into the cart?" he asked.

Lowering her head, Sarah climbed into the back of the cart and dropped down hard enough to make the horse hitched to it shuffle nervously from one leg to another. Cocking her head to one side, she kept her eyes fixed upon Clint and curled her lips into the frown of a little girl who'd just been scolded.

Trying not to laugh at her, Clint made sure Sarah's wrists were still tied and then pulled her legs straight out so he could tie her ankles. All the while, Sarah fretted and grumbled in dissatisfaction with the whole process. When every knot was tied, Clint upset Sarah even more by draping an old blanket over the top of the cart.

"Good Lord!" Sarah groused. "Is that necessary?"

"Stop complaining. You're the only one that gets to ride in the shade." Before Sarah could complain any more, Clint made sure the blanket was in place and then walked away from the cart.

Heather waited near the stable, holding Eclipse's reins in one hand and covering her mouth with the other. Even with her mouth covered, she couldn't hide the fact that she was about to burst out laughing at any moment.

Forcing herself to remain composed, Heather said, "I wasn't sure why you needed that cart. Even now, I can hardly believe it."

"Well, I can't exactly trust her with her own horse, and I don't want to take my chances with her on the back of mine. I'm sure you don't want to try to wrangle her while you're riding."

"So who's going to . . ." Heather cut herself off and glanced nervously toward the cart. Lowering her voice a bit, she asked, "Who's going to drive the cart?"

"I will," Clint replied. "You can ride Eclipse alongside the cart. He'll carry you without needing much direction. I don't think Sarah will get loose, but if she does get around to causing trouble, I want her to get to me first."

The expression on Heather's face was solemn and she shook her head slowly. "You're a gentleman, Clint Adams, but I should drive the cart and you know it."

"I do?"

Heather nodded. "If she gets loose, she'll probably jump out of that cart and make a run for it. You need to be the one to chase after her. If anyone gives us trouble, you need to ride free to take care of things. And if she gets her hands free, the last thing you want is for her to reach out and snatch your gun away."

"Sounds like you've had experience transporting prisoners," Clint said.

"No, but I've got the sense God gave a mule. This isn't too hard to figure out. You just didn't want to ask me to ride so close to her after she already got the jump on me."

Shrugging, Clint admitted, "I thought you might be in a bit of a rough spot with that."

"No rougher than my normal duties in dealing with the patients in their rooms. I can handle myself. If things do go badly, you'll be right there next to me to make sure she doesn't get the upper hand like she and Solomon did before."

"You're sure you want to do this?"

Heather patted Clint's cheek and walked toward the cart. "We already had this conversation and my answer's the same. Let's get moving before Solomon gets too far away from us."

TWENTY-TWO

Clint led the way out of Running Springs while the day was still young. Eclipse was just happy to get moving again, while Heather's horse didn't seem so enthused. It was a brown mare named Edie, who was obviously used to going as far as Rozekiel before getting a rest. Once they'd covered more ground than it would have taken for them to get to the sanitarium, Edie started to huff and stomp at the ground every other step.

"I know how she feels!" Sarah whined from the back of the cart.

Heather looked over her shoulder, but could only see the old blanket that was draped on top of the cart. Since Sarah leaned her back against the cart and stretched her feet out toward the back end, there wasn't much to prop up the blanket. Already, the cover had drooped until the top of Sarah's head could be seen as a bump.

"Well, the both of you just need to put up with it," Heather replied to Edie almost as much as to Sarah. "Because complaining won't do you any good."

Clint made certain to keep as close to the cart as he could. He was glad to see that he didn't need to step in to keep Sarah in line for the moment. When Heather glanced over at him, Clint tipped his hat and motioned for her to commence.

Heather snapped the reins and clucked her tongue, which was enough to square things with the mare pulling the cart. Although Sarah wasn't content with her situation, she shut up about it for the time being.

Following the first instructions Sarah had given, Clint rode north until he was almost a mile out of town. Although he was hesitant to break the silence that had fallen over the little group, Clint pulled back on Eclipse's reins just enough to move to the back of the wagon. He then leaned over and pulled up one corner of the blanket.

"How are you doing in there?" he asked cheerfully.

Sarah glared at him with what could only be described as burning hatred. "Suffocating," she grunted. "Thank you very much."

"It's time for you to earn your keep. Where, exactly, were you going to meet Solomon?"

"I know he was headed north. If you want any more help than that, I'll need to see where we're going."

Nodding slowly as if considering that, Clint said, "I know you and Solomon were in a rush, but don't expect me to believe you two had the sense to bolt from that hotel and split up without agreeing on a spot to meet back up again."

Sarah did a real good job of maintaining a mix of confusion on her otherwise insulted expression. She couldn't keep it up for long, however, when Clint kept staring her in the eye. Finally, she resorted back to her little pout. "You're a good man, Clint. I know you won't keep me from getting fresh air and sunshine."

"I'd be happy to take the cover off the wagon for a while," he replied. "Just as soon as you tell me where you're supposed to meet Solomon."

"We were supposed to ride to a cabin a few miles north of town. It's a spot that's—"

"By the way," Clint interrupted. "If I find out you lied to me, I'll drag you back to the law wrapped up in a bundle and let them know how you bragged to me about all the men you killed during your escape. Also, you won't have a cart beneath you when I do the dragging."

Still frozen in the middle of her sentence, Sarah chewed on her lip and nodded. "We were supposed to head north to a town called Crow's Nest. It's at the end of a trail that leads up toward the mountains, but it's not all the way in the mountains. I think it used to be a mine or something."

Clint smiled and pulled the blanket all the way off the top of the cart. "There, now. That wasn't so hard. Enjoy the day. It looks like it's going to be a nice one."

When he rode up to the front of the cart, Clint set Eclipse's pace to match that of Heather's mare. Behind him, Sarah's contented humming drifted through the air.

"So where are we going?" Heather asked.

"You heard the lady," Clint replied. "The town's called Crow's Nest."

"Do you believe her? I mean, do you honestly think she'd just hand over that much so easily?"

"Would you have preferred I hold her feet to a fire?" Clint asked.

Heather shifted in her seat and glanced nervously over her shoulder. "No, but I thought there'd be more to it than that. I told you . . ." She drifted off as she glanced once more over her shoulder. Although Sarah wasn't looking at her, the redhead was less than a few feet behind the driver's seat.

"I told you she lies," Heather said.

"If I wasn't going to trust her to hold up her end of the deal," Clint said, "I wouldn't have brought her along."

Sarah's humming took on a more victorious tone.

Seeing the urgency in Heather's eyes, Clint leaned forward so she could speak to him in a hurried whisper.

"There might not even be such a place as Crow's Nest," Heather said into Clint's ear.

"That's very true." Raising his voice so anyone in the vicinity could hear it, Clint added, "And if there is no Crow's Nest, I'll just strike off on my own. I sure won't need any extra weight for that, so I'll just dump the cart along with whatever is in it."

Sarah's humming stopped.

TWENTY-THREE

Clint was actually a bit surprised when he rode around a rocky bend and saw the little cluster of buildings situated up on the side of a small cliff face. Because of the stretch of low trail and the sharp rise of the rocks, the cliff looked like a mountain. Upon closer inspection, the top of the cliff couldn't have been more than a hundred feet or so from the lowest spot on the trail that Clint and Heather were navigating. Even so, it was an impressive sight.

"Are we there yet?" Sarah whined from the back of the cart.

"Looks like it," Clint replied.

"You think that's really the place?" Heather asked.

Shrugging, Clint gave his reins a flick and moved farther along the trail until the ground began to wind upward toward the buildings. "There's one way to find out."

The trail quickly narrowed until Eclipse was forced to ride ahead of the cart. Heather gripped her reins hard enough to whiten her knuckles and rode slowly enough to make certain both of the cart's wheels remained on solid ground. Even though Clint knew they could afford to go a bit faster than that, he used the extra time to examine the town they were approaching.

He'd seen plenty of abandoned mining towns and this one looked more like one of those than anything that had people still living in it. The buildings were arranged in a row that stretched all the way along the top of the cliff. From a distance, the town looked as if it truly was perched on top of the rocks like a nest. Once they'd gained some altitude and gotten closer to the town, it was easier to see that the place was built on a long shelf at the top of those cliffs. Because of that, the row of buildings that could be seen from below were the only buildings in town. Crow's Nest was basically half of one street with one hell of a view.

Drawing to a stop before getting any closer to the town, Clint dismounted and walked around to the back of the cart. He'd replaced the blanket to make sure nobody from above could get a look at who was riding in the cart, so he pulled back the makeshift cover to address Sarah.

"Where were you supposed to meet up with Solomon?" Clint asked.

"He was gonna rent a room in a place called the Canteen."

"What name was it under?"

Screwing up her mouth as if she were trying to lock her lips together, Sarah eventually grumbled, "I won't tell you." As soon as she saw the warning glare on Clint's face, she added, "He'll only show himself if he sees me anyway, and he'll run if he sees me dragged around like a prisoner."

Clint nodded slowly and replied, "Then I can't exactly do that."

Sarah straightened and lifted her chin as if she were expecting someone to pat her on the head. That made it even more shocking for her when the blanket was dropped back down unceremoniously onto the cart.

"Keep an eye on her," Clint said to Heather. "There's a good spot right over there by that first building. Drive the cart up to it and set the brake. Then wait for me and we'll go from there."

"What about me?" Sarah asked from under the blanket.

Clint reached under the blanket so he could stuff a bandanna into her mouth. When he walked back around to Heather, he found her looking almost as shocked as Sarah. Taking the rifle from the boot of his own saddle, Clint handed it to Heather and said, "Take this and defend yourself if Solomon or anyone else gives you any trouble."

"But I don't know if I can do that," Heather protested.

"You probably won't have to do anything," Clint told her. "Sarah's tied up tight as a drum and most anyone in this town will be looking more at me than you. Besides, this place is so small that I'll be able to keep an eye on you from wherever I go." Leaning forward so he could rub a comforting hand along her cheek, Clint added, "And I won't be going far."

Heather took the rifle and set it on the seat beside her.

As Clint got back into his saddle and rode toward the town, he could hear the rumble of the cart's wheels behind him. It only took a few minutes for him to reach the town, which was marked by a sign that had been painted onto a piece of rotten wood. Sure enough, the place was called Crow's Nest.

Clint rode tall in his saddle and made certain his jacket was open far enough to show the gun at his side. More than that, he rode with one hand down close to his holster as if he meant to draw at the slightest provocation. As he expected, his entrance drew plenty of glances.

There weren't many folks out and about, but the ones who were there watched Clint intently. Crow's Nest was a quiet little place that couldn't have had more than a dozen families living there. If there wound up being half that number, Clint wouldn't have been too surprised. At any rate, the street was quiet enough for Clint to hear the cart roll to a stop somewhere behind him. When he glanced over his shoulder, he saw Heather setting the brake in the spot he'd asked her to wait.

The Canteen wasn't hard to spot. By the looks of things, it was the only saloon in town and was situated close to the middle of the short stretch of buildings. As Clint approached the Canteen, he took a closer look at the buildings on either side of it. Crow's Nest had been a mining town, all right. That much was easy enough to tell by the signs and lettering on the stores and front windows. Nearly every business in sight had a name or two scratched out and replaced by the title of the current occupant. Even the locals scurried around as if they expected to pick up and leave town at the drop of a hat.

Steeling himself by taking a deep breath and placing his hand upon the grip of his Colt, Clint pushed open the saloon's door and walked straight to the bar.

"How many rooms have you got for rent in here?" Clint asked.

The barkeep took a reflexive step back and replied, "I got plenty and they're the best beds in town."

"How many rooms are already rented?"

"Two. That leaves plenty of space open."

Slapping ten dollars onto the bar, Clint asked, "Would this cover the cost of my room?"

As expected, the barkeep's eyes widened and he reached for the money. "I'll even throw in breakfast and a bath if you want."

Before the barkeep could get to the money, Clint slapped his hand down on the money. When he lifted his hand, there was another ten dollars on the bar. "Keep the room. Tell me which room was rented by a man traveling on his own."

"Short fellow with stubble for hair?"

"Sounds like the one."

"First room at the top of the stairs," the bartender said. "He's probably already seen you, though. He's the squirrelly type."

Clint tipped his hat and left the money on the bar. When he got to the narrow staircase leading to the second floor, he climbed the steps two at a time and reached the top in no time. His eyes had already found the door he was after and his ears had already picked up on the sound of footsteps scrambling inside that room.

TWENTY-FOUR

Clint slammed his boot against the door and forced it open on the first try. The flimsy piece of wood cracked against the wall as Clint rushed into the room.

The room was just big enough to allow the door to swing without hitting the narrow bed that was flush against the opposite wall. In that bed was a slender woman with black hair. She sat bolt upright and desperately tried to gather up enough sheets to cover her naked body before Clint could get a look at her. She didn't succeed.

Although Clint noticed the woman's small, pert breasts, he didn't linger to examine her any closer. Clint was more interested in the man who was already halfway out the window. "Oh, no you don't!" Clint said as he lunged across the room to grab ahold of the man's ankle.

Solomon Reyes had just started to fall outside when he felt Clint snag his leg. With his arms already tangled in his coat and his legs snarled by Clint and the window frame, Solomon couldn't do much more than drop onto the awning and hope for the best. What he got was an awning that was barely strong enough to withstand a stiff breeze, much less the weight of a full-grown man.

All of Solomon's momentum leaping through the window was robbed from him in the blink of an eye. In that instant, he stopped moving forward and found himself dropping straight down until his chest slapped against the side of the saloon. The wall hit him in the face like a board that had been swung at his chin. His arms flapped like the wings of a lame bird as he tried once more to push away from the wall.

Shifting to grab ahold of Solomon's leg with both hands, Clint had to fight to keep from laughing at the man. "You're gonna have to stop kicking," Clint said. When Solomon continued to struggle and flail, Clint shouted, "Hold still unless you want me to drop you on your damn head!"

Solomon's legs stopped squirming, but he continued to scratch at the wall with both hands while stretching his arms as if to reach the ground. When he reached the limits of his flexibility, Solomon started to groan and strain to stretch a little more.

Clint pulled Solomon up until he could reach down and grab the man's belt. Apparently, Solomon had been in a hurry to pull his clothes on because the belt slipped through a few loops before Clint shifted his grip to the waistband of Solomon's pants. While slowly hauling Solomon up, Clint said, "I take it you're Solomon Reyes."

"Who are you?" Solomon shouted. "What do you want from me? Did they send you?"

"I'm bringing you back home, Solomon."

Twisting to look up at the window, Solomon wore an expression that didn't seem to fit on the face of a man dangling over a stretch of cold, rocky ground. "Home?" Solomon asked. "I can go home?" Suddenly, Solomon's eyes narrowed and he bared his teeth. "You're just gonna take me back to Rozekiel! I won't go back there!"

By this time, despite his weak shoulder, Clint just had to lean back and pull one more time to bring Solomon into the room. The short man landed with a *thump* and cracked his head against the window frame along the way. As Solomon flopped around to right himself and grab the lump on his head, Clint looked over to the bed.

The woman with the black hair had pulled on a slip, which didn't cover her much more than the blankets. Her legs were covered, but the top was unbuttoned enough to give Clint a generous view of her cleavage. The chill in the room had caused her nipples to become hard and press against the flimsy material.

"You can go ahead and leave," Clint told her.

The woman placed one hand upon her hip and jabbed a finger toward Solomon. "He still owes me money," she said.

"What?" Solomon grunted. "I was gonna—"

"Five dollars," she cut in.

"Is that true, Solomon?" Clint asked.

Solomon had just managed to sit upright and now he looked like a child who was sitting in a corner after sassing his mother. Playing up to that role perfectly, Solomon scowled and shook his head. "I don't know what she's talking about. This isn't even my room!"

Unable to hold himself back, Clint reached down to grab ahold of Solomon's ankle again. He pulled the other man up again and started shaking as Solomon flapped his arms and scraped his hands against the floor. "Why don't I just keep shaking until this lady's five dollars comes out?" Clint asked.

"No, no!" Solomon cried. "It's in my pocket. Just put me down and I'll get it."

Clint set Solomon down and watched him closely. Grumbling to himself as he stretched his legs out and dug into his pocket, Solomon pulled out some money and tossed it toward her. A few silver dollars landed on the floor and he waved angrily toward her.

"That's all she earned," Solomon grunted. Once he saw the look in Clint's eye along with half a twitch in his direction, Solomon quickly dug into his pockets some more. This time, he kept throwing money until there appeared to be more than enough on the floor at the woman's feet.

"Throwing it at her wasn't very nice," Clint scolded.

The woman stooped down to pick up the money. She was laughing as she said, "It's all right, mister. After that show, I don't mind collecting my own fee. It was nice meeting you, Sol," she said as she straightened up again. "Looks like I won't be seeing you again anytime soon."

"Is that true?" Solomon squeaked. His eyes twitched back and forth between Clint and the woman, who was stepping out of the room. "Are you here to kill me? Is that true? Oh, God."

Now that he had Solomon shaking in his boots. Clint merely had to tug on the man's sleeve to get him to scramble to his feet. "Come along with me, Solomon. I brought along a friend of yours to keep you company on the ride back to Rozekiel."

TWENTY-FIVE

On the way out of the saloon, Solomon had to dig into his pockets one more time to pay what he owed for the room. When he began to object to the barkeep's demands, Solomon cast a nervous glance over his shoulder at Clint and then slapped the money on the bar. "It's all I got left," Solomon grunted.

The barkeep sifted through the coins and replied, "It's enough to settle your bill." After that, he swept up the money and shifted his attention back to his other customers.

Feeling Clint nudge his shoulder, Solomon began trudging toward the door. "I didn't see no badge on you," he said.

"Probably not," Clint replied.

"So you ain't one of Laherty's boys?"

"Nope."

"You a bounty hunter?"

"This will go a lot easier for all of us if you just keep your mouth shut and come along peacefully."

Both of them had stepped outside by now and Solomon was looking around. Apart from a few people walking a bit farther up the street, there was no one else to be seen. Solomon ripped free of Clint's grasp and turned around.

"If you ain't the law and you ain't no bounty hunter, then who the hell are you?" Solomon asked.

Clint walked toward him and reached out to grab Solomon's arm. Before he could get a grip on the other man, Clint was slapped aside.

After landing that first blow, Solomon backed away and held out his arms. "Now what?" he said. "You caught me when I had my back turned and a woman beneath me, but now you don't got the—"

Solomon's challenge was cut short when Clint slapped his hand against the grip of his Colt and said, "If you don't get some sense, I'll be forced to use this. After I clear leather, my trigger finger gets a little itchy."

Staring at Clint, Solomon was obviously sizing him up. He gnawed on his lower lip and shifted from one foot to the other. All the while, Solomon's hands twitched as if he was about to reach for a holster that wasn't there.

"Where are you going to run, Solomon?" Clint asked. "You're not even wearing any boots."

As soon as Solomon looked down at his feet, Clint flew forward and cracked him in the jaw with a quick left fist. Just when it seemed Solomon couldn't be more surprised than by that first punch, the second punch came along to send Solomon staggering backward. Neither of Clint's fists did a lot of damage, but they put Solomon off his game long enough for Clint to move around behind him.

Once he was there, Clint pulled one of Solomon's arms behind his back and pulled it upward until the joint locked and Solomon let out a pained grunt.

"You done with this show?" Clint asked. "Or do you still have some fight left in you?"

"I got plenty of fight in me," Solomon replied. When he felt his arm get pulled up a bit more, he lifted himself onto his tiptoes and added, "But I'll give it a rest for now."

"Good," Clint said as he eased up a bit on the pressure. "I wouldn't want to listen to you grouse about a broken arm all the way back to Running Springs."

Solomon went along easily now that he could feel his elbow was on the verge of snapping. Whenever he tried to say anything, Clint cut him off with a quick twist to the arm that was hooked behind his back. Even though he was frantically looking around for some form of salvation, Solomon quickly turned away from the saloon when he saw the barkeep stepping outside.

"Hey!" the barkeep shouted. "Was Dixie right? Is that fella from that loony bin down in Running Springs?"

Since this wasn't the time for a prolonged explanation, Clint assumed Dixie was the woman who had been in Solomon's room and replied, "Yes, sir, but I'm taking him back there right now."

"You might wanna tell the family of those folks he killed while you're at it. They'll want to hear he's getting what's coming to him."

Clint looked to Solomon, who was gaping at the barkeep. "What family?" Clint asked.

"The one that lives up the trail a stretch. You might wanna keep that animal outta Grant's sight, though. He's liable to tear you apart to get to the one that spilled all of his kin's blood."

"Thank you," Clint said as he tipped his hat. "I might just have to pass by there and let him know what happened here today."

Either the barkeep had heard enough or he had work to do inside, because he gave Clint and Solomon a half-hearted wave as he turned and went back into the saloon. When Clint looked at Solomon again, he found the other man still staring at the saloon with wide, unblinking eyes.

"Is that true?" Clint asked.

"What?"

"Don't play dumb with me. I'm in no mood for it."

Solomon shook himself out of his trance and fixed his eyes on Clint. He'd been almost motionless before, but now he couldn't stop shaking his head and squirming in Clint's grasp. "I didn't kill no one! Not for a long time!"

"What the hell's that supposed to mean?"

"All I did was get away from Rozekiel as quick as I could. I hid in the trees for a while, met up with Sarah, and then we split up to come here. I used the money I was given to buy some whiskey and you made me give the rest away! Honest!"

"What about that family the bartender was talking about?" Seeing the dazed expression on Solomon's face, Clint shoved him down the street. "I'll find out for myself."

Although Solomon tried to speak a few times, Clint wasn't hearing any of it. All he wanted to do was get back to Heather and wrap up Solomon for his trip back to the sanitarium. While he was at it, he figured he'd double-check Sarah's wrappings as well.

Unfortunately, when Clint got back to the cart, Heather and Sarah were nowhere in sight.

TWENTY-SIX

The cart wasn't just overturned. It was nearly torn to pieces. One wheel was lying on the ground a few feet away and the other was busted so badly that it would never be used again. The cart itself was missing one side, but that wasn't what worried Clint the most. He was more concerned with the blood staining the driver's seat.

"What the hell happened here, Solomon?" Clint snarled as he wheeled around to face the man. When Solomon tried to look away, Clint spun him so there was nowhere else for him to look. "Talk to me!"

Solomon shook his head so vigorously that it was in danger of snapping off. "I didn't do this! I was upstairs in bed. All I wanted was some pussy. It's been so long since—"

"Don't talk to me about that!" Shoving Solomon toward the wrecked cart as if he were pushing a dog's nose into his own mess, Clint said, "Tell me about this."

"It . . . It must have been him," Solomon replied.

"Who?"

"Creed! It was Creed!"

Clint didn't believe anything Solomon was saying, but he knew he didn't have time to continue the conversation long enough to get to the truth. Shoving Solomon in front of him, Clint rushed back to where he'd hitched Eclipse and took the rope hanging from the saddle.

"What are you doing?" Solomon asked as the rope was lashed around his wrists.

After having tied so many knots lately, Clint was getting awfully good at the task. He had Solomon's hands bound behind his back in the space of a few seconds. "I'm going after Sarah and you're coming along with me."

"But I didn't even see her. Do you know where they went?"

"There's only two ways for them to go up here," Clint replied as he hoisted Solomon onto Eclipse's back. "Since I didn't hear any commotion around the saloon, I'm putting my money they went the other direction." He then climbed into the saddle and got himself situated so Solomon was mostly secure behind him. "If you squirm or cause any trouble, I'll drop you on your head. Understand me?"

"What am I supposed to do back here? My hands aren't even free!"

"Then I hope you've got some good balance." With that, Clint snapped the reins and got Eclipse moving. He could feel Solomon shifting behind him, but the other man was too busy trying to keep from breaking his neck to cause any trouble. Fortunately, the trail was fairly level and sloped downward once Crow's Nest was behind them. That way, Solomon could lean forward against Clint's back and hope his legs were strong enough to keep him in place.

Clint's gamble paid off.

Just as he was starting to think he'd made the wrong bet, Clint spotted some dust being kicked up a little ways down the trail. Since the way up the rocky slope to Crow's Nest was steep and jagged, it wasn't the sort of ride that could be taken quickly. If not for that, the horse in front of him could have been long gone before it had been spotted.

"Hang on!" Clint said as he flicked his reins and urged Eclipse to go just a bit faster.

Solomon was about to protest when he felt the Darley Arabian picking up speed beneath him. Rather than waste his breath on words, Solomon clenched his legs as tightly as he could around Eclipse's back and leaned as much weight as possible against Clint's shoulders. It wasn't a good arrangement, but it was the best he could manage.

From his vantage, Clint could see at least two figures riding on the horse ahead of him. But those figures weren't the only things weighing that animal down. There was also a large bundle lying across the horse's rump. As that horse continued to work its way down the slope, Clint swore he saw that bundle move.

Eclipse took the steep descent like he was born in the mountains. Even when his hooves skidded against some loose gravel or slipped on some bare rock, he simply shifted his weight and used his momentum to keep negotiating the trail. Clint kept his eye on the horse ahead of him and let Eclipse do the rest.

Suddenly, a scream ripped through the air. Not only did it catch Clint's attention, but he even thought he recognized the voice of the person who was doing the screaming. "Heather!" he shouted. "Is that you?"

"Clint! Clint, help me!"

Once he heard that, Clint saw that the bundle on the back of the other horse was a body wrapped almost as tight as Sarah had been for most of the ride to Crow's Nest. After Eclipse had closed some of the distance between them, Clint could make out the legs that were extended from the bundle and kicking wildly.

The figure holding on to the one that gripped the other horse's reins turned around to glance in Clint's direction. That figure was wearing a hat, but the wind caught its rim at a new angle and flipped the hat into the air to allow a mess of red hair to flow freely around the figure's head. Sarah turned around and extended one arm toward Clint. A second later, a gunshot cracked through the air.

Clint reflexively ducked as a bullet whipped several feet to the right of his head.

"Jesus!" Solomon yelped as he twitched and nearly flopped off Eclipse's back. "Who's shooting at us?"

"Your friend the redhead," Clint replied as he drew his Colt and took aim.

"Sarah? That crazy bitch!"

Another shot hissed past Clint. This one was a little closer to its target. "I think she heard that," he warned. Clint sighted along the Colt's barrel and almost pulled his trigger when he felt a flicker of pain in his wounded shoulder. Between the cold air, all the day's drama, and the strength required to hold the pistol out and keep it steady, that wound was flaring up and sending jolts of pain all the way down his arm. It wasn't nearly enough pain to keep Clint from firing, but it was enough to make him pause before taking a shot that had an outside chance of hitting Heather.

Clint adjusted his aim a bit and squeezed his trigger. The modified Colt barked once and caused the horse's rider to duck and steer a bit to the left. Since that was exactly what Clint had been hoping for, he steadied his aim and waited for his next opportunity to shoot.

Sarah twisted around and fired a few more rounds, but none of them came close to hitting anything other than a few unlucky trees. As she continued to shift and turn in her saddle, Sarah moved enough to give Clint a few fleeting glances at the man holding the other horse's reins. All Clint could see in those few glimpses, however, was a set of broad shoulders and a head covered in closely cropped hair similar to Solomon's.

Firing once more to the other rider's left, Clint waited until that horse veered to the right before firing again. This

time, he sent a bullet hissing through the air close enough
to that rider's right ear to make him pull his reins in the opposite direction.

Now that he was approaching a bend in the trail, Clint
was forced to pull back on his reins before Eclipse was
given a bit more than he could handle. The Darley Arabian
had done well so far, but there was no reason to push it.
Now that the other horse didn't seem to know which way to
go, Clint was fairly certain he could catch up to Sarah before they got away from him.

Clint took aim and prepared to fire a shot that would clip
the arm of the man on the other horse. Before he could pull
his trigger, he saw Sarah turn back around and shove Heather
off the horse's back. Heather's screams ripped through the
air and were followed by the crunch of her body landing on
the trail.

TWENTY-SEVEN

While Clint had previously been careful to keep Eclipse at a speed that wouldn't put him at risk, he now pushed the Darley Arabian to his limits so he could get to the spot where Heather had landed. Even though he hadn't seen Heather's face, Clint knew she was the one wrapped up in that bundle. He'd heard her voice before and now he prayed to hear it again.

"Heather!" Clint shouted as he drew closer to her. "I'm coming. Can you hear me?"

The bundle was quiet. It was also very still, which sent a worried chill through Clint's whole body.

Once he got close enough to the bundle, Clint jumped down from the saddle. Eclipse knew to stop as soon as Clint had dismounted and fussed noisily as Solomon continued to squirm and fight to stay on the stallion's back.

Even though he was only a few steps away from the bundle, Clint felt as if he had to cover several miles before he got to it. It looked as if the blanket that had been used to cover the cart on the way into town was now wrapped around Heather's body. Clint could see her legs sticking out from the blanket as he knelt down to get her out of it.

The only way for him to get her free was to unroll the

blanket a ways. Since the blanket was wrapped so tightly around her, his hopes of getting her out safely sank even further. A good amount of hope returned, however, when he heard a groan as he rolled her onto her back.

Heather's head emerged from the top of the blanket, but her face was at an awkward angle and her neck must have been stretched as far as it could go. Her face was battered and cut, but her eyes came open and her lips strained to push out a few words.

"Clint?" she moaned. "Is that . . . ?"

"It's me, Heather," he said. "Are you hurt?"

"I don't . . . think so."

"Let me know if this hurts you."

As soon as she felt the blanket around her loosen, Heather started to struggle even harder. Her eyes brightened the moment she was able to move one of her arms. "Get me out of this," she said with a hint of panic in her voice.

Clint didn't want to make the situation worse if she'd broken anything in the fall, but he knew he wasn't about to keep her still. Once he was able to make some slack in the blanket, he pulled it away from her and kept her on top of it. Her face was dirty and her clothes were ripped, but Heather seemed to be coming around pretty quickly.

After she felt Clint's hand brush against her cheek, she shook her head and sat up. "What happened?" she asked. Wincing in pain, Heather allowed Clint to ease her back down. "Where's Creed?"

"If you mean the fellow that was riding that horse," Clint said as he looked down the trail, "he got away."

TWENTY-EIGHT

Sarah kept herself twisted around so she could watch Heather as long as possible after shoving her off the horse's back. Even after she was too far away to see Heather or Clint, Sarah kept looking as if she expected some sort of encore.

"Is that lawman still following us?" the man holding the reins asked.

"No," Sarah replied with a definite hint of disappointment in her voice. "Looks like he stopped to pick up that nurse."

"Nurse," the man scoffed. "That's a hell of a stretch for any of them bitches at Rozekiel. Even though she wasn't one of the bad ones, I still should'a broke her neck."

"If you did that, she wouldn't have held that other fella off for so long."

The man turned around to get a look at the trail behind him. His face was scarred and his hair grew in irregular clumps. His expression had an equal mix of disgust and amusement as he studied the ground he was leaving behind. Once he was convinced there was nobody behind him, he put on an ugly grin and turned back around to face the trail ahead. "That was a real good idea to keep her alive," he said.

"He's the sort that will tend to the wounded long enough to give us plenty of time to get away from here."

"Who said we was goin' away?"

Having settled in with her arms around the man's midsection and her cheek resting against his shoulder, Sarah blinked and said, "Well, we sure aren't going back."

"I can't abide havin' no man follow me. Who was he anyways?"

"His name's Clint Adams and he's not a lawman. He's just some gunman who was out and about at the wrong time."

The man holding the reins gritted his teeth as if he were literally chewing on what he'd heard. As he did that, the muscles in his face twitched enough to make his scars twitch. "He was just there?"

"I don't know why he was there. It doesn't even matter."

The man pulled back on the reins so hard that the horse nearly lost its footing before it stopped. The animal tried to keep going so it could slow at a more natural pace, but the man only pulled the reins harder until the horse finally stopped. Before they'd come to a halt, the man twisted around and screamed into Sarah's face like a wild animal.

"You don't tell me what matters and what don't!" he snapped. Sarah started to defend herself, but the man kept on screaming at her. "I got us out of that hellhole, not you! I killed them guards and found them holes in the wall, not you!"

"I know, Jonas. I know," Sarah said in a soothing, yet trembling voice.

For a second, it seemed Jonas was just as close to kissing her as he was to beating her down. The more breaths he took, the calmer he became. Finally, he let out a breath and blinked a few times as if he were just waking up from a nap.

"That was a good idea to dump that nurse off like that," he said. "Let's get ourselves somewhere safe."

Happy to see that side of him return, Sarah wrapped her arms around his waist and nodded. "I still got the money Solomon stole for us, so we can get a real room with a real bed."

Jonas snapped his reins and leaned forward as his horse built up speed. They rode for miles along stretches of trail that seemed narrower than the horse's body. During those times, Sarah gripped him tighter and closed her eyes until the horse's stride became smoother and its hooves weren't clattering against rock.

They kept the mountains to their left as they rode north. The sun never got too high, which meant the day never got too warm. If he felt any of the chill, Jonas didn't give a sign. Even when the horse seemed ready to slow down and take a breath, he kept whipping its sides until the animal had no choice but to keep running.

Sarah didn't open her eyes until she felt the horse come to a sudden, shaky stop. When she opened her eyes, she looked around as if she were expecting to see guns pointed at them or a posse circling around to cut them off. All she saw was a short stretch of buildings and the cloud of dust that had been kicked up by Jonas's sudden halt.

"Stay out here and keep watch on the horse," he said as he dropped down from the saddle.

Sliding off the horse, Sarah hurried around to step in front of him before he could enter a squat building marked as a hotel. She placed her hands upon his chest and started rubbing him as soon as she saw the fire in his eyes. "Maybe I should go in," she said.

When Sarah's hands drifted up to his face, Jonas snarled and swatted them away. "Why? You think I'm too dumb to rent a room?"

"No, no," she quickly replied. "I just think that . . ." She pulled her hands back, but her eyes drifted to the small, circular scars that dotted both sides of Jonas's head. "Men are after us and someone might recognize you."

"They might recognize us both."

"I've got the money and besides . . . I may be able to sweet-talk us into a deal for the price of a room."

Jonas's lips curled into a gruesome smile as he nodded. "You might just be able to do that. Go on and get us a room, but be quick about it. I got plans for you, darlin'."

She giggled and turned to rush into the hotel.

Jonas watched her until she disappeared through the doorway. As he turned to look up and down the street, his hand drifted to a gun that was stuck beneath his belt. His other hand went up to the freshest of the scars, which was positioned just behind his left ear. He winced when he touched the tender flesh and let out a noisy grunt of a breath.

"What the hell you lookin' at?" he snarled to a local woman.

The woman averted her eyes as quickly as she could and ducked into the closest store.

When Jonas lowered his left hand, there was fresh blood on his fingertips.

again when I heard someone ride up to the cart. I looked over and it was Jonas."

"Who's Jonas?" Clint asked.

"Jonas Creed," she replied. "He's another patient from Rozekiel."

Upon hearing that, Clint looked over his shoulder at Solomon. Sure enough, Solomon was shifting uncomfortably and doing his best not to look anywhere near Clint's face. Putting away that bit of knowledge for the moment, Clint said, "Go on."

"Creed has killed more people than anyone truly knows about," Heather said. "Every time we asked him about it, he would give us a different number. When we tried to look into court records and figures kept from where he used to live, we just kept finding more bodies. The trail started with his own family and just spread out from there."

"From what I've heard, that trail leads up to a homestead not too far from here," Clint said. As he spoke, he watched Solomon's face. "You know anything about that?" he asked him.

Solomon shook his head.

"Maybe I should check on it myself," Clint said.

"And so should I," Heather added. "I was there when Dr. Wolcott spoke to Creed. I know how he . . . how he liked to kill." Looking at the man behind her, she added, "I heard a lot about all of the doctor's patients."

Clint helped her down before Solomon could try anything and led her to the cold water of the stream.

THIRTY

The hotel was a drafty old building that had obviously started out as a barn. There were two rooms sectioned off by planks that looked to be newer than the rest of the structure and another two rooms upstairs in a loft that still had straw scattered on the floor. Sarah led Jonas through the front half of the hotel and into one of the rooms in the back of the main floor.

There was an old four-poster that leaned to one side, a dresser that was missing half its drawers, and a barrel that had been sawed in half and filled with mostly clean water. As soon as he was inside, Jonas dropped his saddlebag on the floor and kicked the door shut with his heel.

Sarah practically skipped over to the barrel so she could bend at the waist and splash one hand in the water.

"Get your clothes off," Jonas snarled. "Right now."

Keeping her back to him, Sarah straightened up and slowly unbuttoned her dress. When she heard the footsteps coming up behind her, she smiled and leaned her head back. Jonas closed the distance between her and the door in a few rushed steps. Now he was close enough to breathe on the back of her neck.

Although Sarah was still doing her best to tempt him by

peeling her dress down from her shoulders, she wasn't moving fast enough for Jonas. He grabbed her bodice and tore it off her with so much force that it probably would have come off even if she hadn't touched a button. Reaching around to grab hold of her breast with one hand, Jonas used his other hand to pull open the front of his pants.

Sarah leaned back and gasped breathlessly while stripping off her dress the rest of the way. It fell down easily once she'd loosened the skirt. Her rounded hips wriggled in expectation and she moved them back until she felt Jonas's erection against her buttocks.

"I waited too long for this," he said as he bent her over and slapped her backside.

Still giggling, Sarah spread her legs apart and grabbed on to the barrel as she closed her eyes and waited to feel him enter her. She only had to wait a few seconds before Jonas's cock slid against her thighs and slipped between the wet lips of her pussy.

As soon as he was inside her, Jonas grabbed on to her hips with both hands and began pounding into Sarah. When he felt her start to straighten up, he placed a hand on the small of her back and held her down so he could continue pounding into her even harder.

Although Sarah was no longer giggling, she was enjoying herself so much that she grabbed the barrel and let out a powerful moan as her first orgasm shot through her body. It was a quick jolt that shook her until it was over. Before she could catch her breath, she felt Jonas slip out of her.

He grabbed her and spun her around so he could take in the sight of her naked body with hungry eyes. His mouth hung open like a wolf that was about to sink its teeth into fresh meat. Jonas reached out to hold her breasts and run his callused hands down toward her stomach.

Sarah challenged him with her eyes and reached down

to stroke his penis. When she felt her wetness on him, she rubbed until his cock became even more rigid in her hand.

Jonas didn't sit still for much more of that before grabbing her and setting her on the edge of the barrel. Her weight caused the barrel to tip, but soon her legs were wrapped around Jonas's waist and he was cupping her buttocks in both hands. From there, he lifted her up and positioned her so his cock was once again pressing against her moist pussy. While pumping his hips forward a bit, he pulled her close until he was once again impaling her.

Sarah wrapped her arms around him so her fingers laced together behind his neck. With her legs still locked around his waist, she could lean back and grind her hips in time to Jonas's pumping so she could make sure his erection slid up into just the right spot. Once Jonas hit that spot, Sarah let her head fall back and arched her back as another orgasm ripped through her.

This time, Jonas could feel her climax as well. Every muscle in her body tensed and her hold on him tightened in every way. He was even able to walk across the room with her attached to him, and she didn't even begin to slip from her spot. Once he got her backed against a wall, he could drive into her with even more powerful thrusts.

Leaning her head forward to rest upon Jonas's shoulder, Sarah held on and moaned into his ear as he pumped furiously between her legs. Jonas tightened his grip on her buttocks and pulled her toward him every time he thrust forward. Their bodies met in a loud impact that was made even louder by Jonas's grunts and Sarah's moans.

Soon, Jonas slowed down so he could catch his breath. Only then did Sarah open her eyes and try to form words instead of breathless groans.

"Don't stop," she gasped. "Don't stop."

Jonas carried her away from the wall and lowered her onto the bed. Once her backside touched the mattress, he dropped her onto the blankets and pulled her legs until she was perched on the edge of the mattress. Sarah grinned and squirmed to accommodate him. She lifted her legs up and placed one ankle on Jonas's shoulder. Before she could set the other ankle down, Sarah felt his hand clamp around it as he fit himself inside of her.

Once Jonas got going again, he wasn't going to be stopped. He pounded into her again and again. Soon, he leaned forward to place his hands upon her breasts as he raced toward his own climax.

Sarah put her hands on top of his and drove the back of her head into the mattress while urging him to grab her even harder. Her legs spread open wide and her hips pumped in time to his thrusts until she saw Jonas glare down at her with the snarl of a wild animal. That sight alone was enough to push her into another orgasm and she was still trembling after he'd exploded inside of her.

"Damn." Jonas sighed. "It's been too long."

"It sure has," Sarah replied as her eyes flickered with a hungry fire. "And you better not make me wait too long for the next one."

THIRTY-ONE

Clint followed the few tracks he could find that led away from the spot where he'd last seen Sarah and Jonas. Since that didn't take much time, he headed back to Crow's Nest with the intention of either repairing the cart that had been broken during Sarah's escape or possibly buying something to replace it. Before he could find the cart or the town, something found them.

"Edie?" Heather said from her spot in the saddle behind Clint. Stretching her neck and leaning forward, she became so excited that she nearly shoved Clint completely off Eclipse's back. "It is Edie! I'd know that girl anywhere!"

Clint squinted at the spot where Heather was pointing and saw a familiar brown mare grazing at a patch of grass that sprouted between two boulders just off the trail. As soon as Heather's voice reached her, Edie snapped her head up and pricked her ears.

"Now that's what I call lucky," Clint said.

Heather swung down from the saddle and hit the ground running. "It's not luck. My Edie would never leave me behind."

"So Edie's that horse's name?" Solomon asked from behind Eclipse.

Keeping one hand on the rope that was tied to his saddle horn, Clint followed that rope all the way back to where it was looped around Solomon's wrists. They hadn't ridden for too long, but Solomon hadn't ridden at all. Instead, he'd run behind Eclipse and prayed the stallion didn't break into a trot.

"It's the horse's name," Clint said.

Solomon nodded and said, "Good. Maybe then I won't have to run like a damned dog anymore."

"You can ride just as soon as you earn your keep."

"I ain't tried to run away once," Solomon whined. "You already set eyes on Creed and let Sarah get away. What the hell else do you want from me?"

"I want you to tell me where Creed's going."

But Solomon was already shaking his head before Clint finished his statement. "Nobody knows where Jonas Creed goes. Hell, I bet Jonas Creed don't even know where he's headed."

"What was the plan after you escaped from that sanitarium?" Clint asked.

"To meet up at Crow's Nest! That was all the plan we had time to make!"

Clint shifted so he could look ahead of Eclipse instead of behind him. Heather had already gotten to the brown mare and was leading it by the reins that still dangled from Edie's neck.

"She's still got her saddle!" Heather said cheerfully.

"Good," Clint replied. "You can scout ahead while I drag this one behind me."

"To hell with that!" Solomon hollered.

"Then tell me where to find Jonas Creed! I'm not going to take the time to haul you all the way back to Rozekiel, and I'm not about to let you sit in a room when you should be helping to clean up the mess you and the rest of those patients made. Help me now or I'll tie you to a tree and let you freeze until the wolves come sniffing around for their next meal."

"And what if I do help?" Solomon asked. "What do I get? And don't tell me I'll get a pardon or an easier sentence when the law starts handing out their verdicts. I may be crazy, but I know you can't promise much in any of them regards."

"What do you want?" Clint asked.

After taking a moment, Solomon said, "I want some hot meals and a big, soft bed to sleep in. And I want dessert! When I get my meals I want a good dessert!"

"That's it?"

"That's plenty. After the slop they serve at Rozekiel and whatever garbage they'll hand out in jail, this'll be the best payment any man could get."

Clint pretended to think it over, but he'd already made his decision. "And if you get these things, you'll lead me to Creed?"

"As best I can."

"That sounds—"

Before Clint could finish, Solomon started hissing and shaking his head to cut him short. "And I don't walk anywhere! I'll ride like any man."

"You'll ride like a man who's still got his hands and feet tied up," Clint amended. "That's the best I'm going to offer with that."

"It's a deal."

Heather rode her mare up to stand beside Eclipse and said, "I thought you two already had this all worked out."

"Things change," Solomon said proudly. "We got a better deal now." Walking up to Clint, he said, "And I'll need some help getting into the saddle, if you please."

"First tell me where we're going," Clint said.

"Go to the first place where Creed and that redheaded bitch can be alone," Solomon replied. "They were all over each other anytime they could manage it back at the sanitarium, but they never got enough time to really get down to business."

"What?" Heather squawked. "I was one of the people in charge of that entire floor and we would never allow male and female patients to socialize that way!"

Solomon chuckled and told her, "You didn't allow it, but they socialized plenty. Sometimes, that redhead would bring some food up to Jonas and she'd fuck him for as long as none of you nurses were watching. Sometimes, she'd just suck his—"

"All right," she said quickly. "That's enough."

Clint didn't have too hard of a time in deciding whether or not to believe Solomon's claim. "I know which way they went from here," he said. "Heather, keep your eyes open for Creed's horse or a spot that might suit his purpose. I want to check in on someone else who might have heard something we can use."

THIRTY-TWO

The homestead wasn't far from Crow's Nest, but it was at the end of a serpentine trail that made the ride seem twice as long as it truly was. Clint had barely spotted the place before a shot cracked through the air and hissed over their heads.

"Is that Creed?" Heather asked nervously.

Clint shook his head. "No. That was just a warning shot."

"How can you be sure?"

"Because it came from a rifle and could have hit either of us if the person firing it had wanted to. At the least, it would have come a whole lot closer to us than that. Just to be safe, you'd better stay here." Looking over his shoulder at Solomon, Clint added, "You too."

"I ain't gonna run like a dog," Solomon groaned. As soon as another shot was fired from the homestead, Solomon couldn't slide off Eclipse's back fast enough. "You know best, I suppose."

Clint rode slowly forward and stopped once he reached the spot where the trail opened up a bit at the front of the little house. Holding his hands up, he shouted, "I'm looking for the Grant place."

An old man stepped forward. He held an old hunting rifle to one shoulder and sighted along its barrel with a wide eye. "I'm Grant and this is my place," he snapped. "What's your business here?"

"My name's Clint Adams. I heard you had some trouble here not too long ago."

"Yeah. So?"

"I'm after the man who gave you that trouble."

Grant took a few more steps around his house, which wasn't much more than a large cabin. A rickety fence enclosed a space to the right of the house, but there were no animals penned in there. In fact, the old man seemed to be the only thing moving apart from Clint and the others he'd brought along with him.

A skinny man who looked to be in his sixties, Grant carried himself with the strength of someone who'd weathered plenty of storms. There was enough fire in his eyes to make it even money if he would pull his trigger or not. "You think it was just one man?" he asked.

"Yes, sir," Clint replied. "One man who was a little taller than you, with short hair and crazy eyes."

As soon as he heard that, Grant lowered his rifle. "He did have crazy eyes. Crazy as the day is long. I ain't never seen anything quite like it."

Clint hadn't actually gotten a close look at Creed's eyes, but he'd looked into the eyes of plenty of killers in his time. He'd also been forced to stare down a few of the patients at Rozekiel, and he knew all too well that whatever demons they had inside of them could be seen just fine through their eyes. From what he'd heard about Jonas Creed, Clint was certain that that one had plenty of demons.

"You mind if I have a word with you, sir?" Clint asked.

"If you're after that murdering son of a bitch, you can have more'n one word. And you can also call me Grant."

Clint dismounted and walked forward. He saw Grant's

eyes dart to the gun at his side, but the old man didn't seem too put off by it. "What happened here, Grant?"

Letting out a breath that seemed to have aged him by twenty years, Grant replied, "I hardly even know what happened. Me and my wife was asleep. The little ones were put to bed long before then."

"Little ones?"

"Two of 'em," Grant said. "A boy and a girl. Their names were . . ." Grant's face took on the qualities of cold rock, but he was obviously fighting to keep that hardness from cracking. His eyes reddened around the edges and he angrily swiped at them with the back of one hand. Turning to stomp toward his front porch, Grant said, "Boy and a girl. Neither of 'em older than ten years."

Following the old man to the porch, Clint lowered himself onto a seat next to the rocker that Grant settled into. He leaned forward with his elbows upon his knees and waited quietly for Grant to continue.

"We didn't hear nothin'," the old man said. "Leastways, I didn't hear nothin' until the door was kicked in."

Clint glanced toward the door and noticed that the hinges were shinier than any other piece of metal to be seen. "There was just the one man?" he asked.

"Yep. He kicked in the door and I charged him like a damn bull. I ain't as strong as I used to be, otherways I would've done some good. As it was, that asshole hit me in the face and kicked me in the ribs till I stayed down. The missus hit him with a pot or pan, but that didn't do no good. He cut her throat and moved straight on to the little ones."

Grant pulled in a breath and held it for a second. Although he was maintaining his stony facade, his eyes remained fixed to a spot on the ground a few feet in front of him. His voice sounded as if it were drifting in from several miles away. "He cut the boy up first, since the boy came runnin' straight toward him. There's only the one door, you see, and the window in the back of the house just got new glass. He tossed a rock through the old glass and I said I'd tan his hide if he busted it again."

Wincing at that, Grant clamped his jaw shut and tightened his grip upon the arms of his chair. Even though Clint wanted to comfort the old man, he knew there wasn't anything he could do to ease that kind of pain.

After finally letting out his breath, Grant said, "The boy put up a fight, but it didn't do any good. Fact is, I think the crazy bastard liked it. He smiled and beat the child to a pulp. Then he moved on to the girl. I thought he might . . . hurt her worse . . . so I tried to fight some more. I could barely move, but he beat me some more and killed the girl quick. I may go to hell for sayin' so, but I think that was the best thing for her." Wincing again, Grant added, "The best if any of this had to happen."

"I know what you're saying," Clint told him. "It sounds like you did as much as you could."

"I hit him. My wife hit him. But it looked like he already got hurt plenty before he even got here."

"What do you mean?"

Grant shifted his eyes toward Clint and kept them there. Even though he was looking at Clint, the old man seemed to be looking through him. "He had scars all along here," he said while waving his hands above both ears. "I thought he was shot. He didn't even twitch when he was hit. Even when I came at him or the missus cracked him in the skull with her pan, that fella didn't even budge. Maybe he ain't even human. If you're going after that bastard, you should know that."

"I appreciate you telling me," Clint said.

Suddenly, Grant lunged toward Clint and grabbed his wrist. The move was so quick that it nearly caused Clint to reach for his gun out of pure reflex.

"Are you going after this bastard?" Grant asked.

"Yes."

"Then you must'a come here for a reason. You need to know what you're after? You're after a man that don't feel no pain and has got no remorse. He's a damned monster. You want my help? I can tell you that fighting him's just a waste of time. You gotta put him down and don't think twice about it. You flinch once and he'll kill you. I don't care how many men you fought before, this one won't stop unless he's dead!"

"Do you know what he was after?" Clint asked. "Where he was going? What he wanted?"

Grant shook his head slowly and eased back into his chair. "He just wanted to kill. He wasn't in no hurry to go nowhere. All he wanted was to kill."

After that, Grant didn't say much of anything.

THIRTY-THREE

Clint rode ahead of Heather and carried Solomon along with him. Eclipse adjusted to the extra weight pretty quickly, but needed some more time to get used to Solomon's constant squirming. After a while, the Darley Arabian just kept moving as if he didn't care whether his new rider stayed on or fell off. Clint felt pretty much the same way.

"If you don't care about finding Creed, then let's just get someplace where we can eat," Solomon groaned.

"What makes you think I'm not interested in finding Creed?" Clint asked.

"For one thing, we haven't gone fast enough to catch a damned rabbit all day long. How do you expect to track down a man?"

"Creed isn't running from us."

Solomon chuckled and looked back at Heather. The slender blonde stared straight back at him with a scolding expression that forced Solomon to turn right around again.

"Sarah's still with him," Solomon pointed out. "She'll be telling him to run just like she must've already told him that you were the man coming after him."

"You think he's afraid of me?" Clint asked.

"He ain't afraid of no man."

"And if he was set to run away, would he have taken the time to rip apart that old man's family?"

Furrowing his brow as he sifted through that, Solomon finally said, "I suppose not."

"I've tracked plenty of men," Clint told him. "Sometimes you need to look for what they leave behind or what they disturb along the way. Other times, you need to rely on other folks to point you in the right direction. Sometimes, all you need to know is the man you're after."

"If you knew Creed, you wouldn't go after him at all."

"Maybe not, but it's too late to turn back now. I've seen too much of what he's done and I can't allow him to do it to anyone else."

"All right, then," Solomon grumbled. "It's your funeral."

"You said Creed couldn't keep his hands off that redhead?" Clint asked.

Solomon let out a sneering laugh. "He took what he could get, but it was Sarah that mostly started pawing at him. I know, 'cause I was sometimes in the room with 'em and they didn't even notice. Either that, or they didn't care if I was there or not."

"That's disgusting," Heather said. "Either I or one of the other nurses was always checking on the patients."

"I know. That's why they had to be so quick about it."

Heather sighed and shook her head. By the looks of it, she didn't want to have much to do with the conversation any longer.

"What would Sarah want to do now that she's free?" Clint asked.

After thinking for a second, Solomon replied, "She'd be the one to get as far away from here as possible. I think she had some family in New York."

Clint shook his head slowly. "What about you, Heather? Can you think of anything that might help?"

Without hesitating, she said, "Jonas wouldn't be sleeping outside."

Looking over his shoulder at her, Clint asked, "Are you sure?"

She nodded. "Every room in the sanitarium was specifically fitted with a window. It was part of the new outlook where the patients were to be exposed to the fresh air and sunlight whenever possible. The rooms that didn't have windows before had windows built in, but Jonas wouldn't have it. He couldn't sleep in a room with a window, even when it wasn't large enough for a child to crawl through."

"Why?"

"You'd have to ask Dr. Wolcott for his theories, but I know he was very adamant about it. Jonas was fine during the day or when he was awake, but he wouldn't sleep if he could see the sky. Sometimes, he wouldn't even go outside when the rest of the patients were given their time in the yard or in the garden so they could—"

"All right," Clint said as a way to cut her off as gently as possible. "If you're sure about it, that's all I need to know."

Heather kept nodding and didn't seem to take any offense at to being interrupted. Her time with all those doctors had gotten her accustomed to much worse behavior. "I'm sure all right," was all she said.

"Damn," Solomon grunted. "Every room *but* mine had a window?"

THIRTY-FOUR

Although Solomon and Heather spent a good portion of the ride into town arguing about Rozekiel policies and food quality, those two had done more than enough to guide Clint in his search for the missing patients. Creed's trail went cold fairly soon after the spot where Clint had lost sight of them, but he knew enough to point him in the right direction.

First of all, Clint knew they were heading north.

Secondly, he knew that Sarah was with him so Creed would be in a rush to get somewhere he could spend some time with her. Knowing Sarah fairly well himself, Clint was certain the redhead wouldn't make it easy for Creed to wait to get his hands on her.

Third, Clint was fairly certain that Creed would prefer to be inside when he did get his hands on Sarah. If he had some aversion to open spaces, that would only leave some sort of hotel or other building for them to hole up in. If Creed couldn't wait and stopped somewhere off the trail, Clint was certain he could pick up a trace of where they'd gone.

Since the land was mostly full of rocks and trees with

bare branches, there weren't a lot of places for two people and a horse to hide for very long. Clint rode slowly enough for him to hear any hooves clattering against rock or dry branches being snapped. He also watched for any movement along the trail that could give away someone's position.

It wasn't a foolproof plan, but it brought Clint to the small town that looked like it had once been another mining camp or even a large homestead. If he had any doubts that Creed or Sarah were in that town, they were erased by the gunshots that were fired at Clint within seconds of him riding down the town's street.

"Jesus!" Solomon yelped from his spot behind Clint. "Get me down from here before I get my head blown off!"

Pulling back on Eclipse's reins, Clint felt the man behind him slide off the horse before he even came to a stop. Clint looked back to make sure Solomon hadn't broken his neck and found the man rolling away like a large, panicked worm. "Stay with him," he told Heather. "Both of you keep down!"

Clint trusted that they would both value their lives enough to follow his orders. He drew his Colt and tapped his heels against Eclipse's sides to get the Darley Arabian charging through the middle of town. A few people jumped out of his way to clear the street, but the first shots that had been fired did a good job of that on their own.

More shots blazed through the air. As those bullets whipped past him, Clint narrowed down their source to two buildings: one was a blacksmith's shop and the other was a place that looked like a barn, but was marked as a hotel. Considering what he'd already been told about Creed, Clint focused his sights upon the latter.

Clint pulled back hard on the reins and swung his leg

over Eclipse's back. That way, he could drop down from the saddle without forcing the stallion to break his stride. Once his boots touched the ground, Clint gave Eclipse's rump a slap and sent the Darley Arabian toward the next corner.

Pushing open the hotel's door with his shoulder, Clint stepped inside and swung his Colt around to cover anyone who might be waiting for him. All he found was a frightened clerk behind the front desk. "Who fired those shots?" Clint asked.

The clerk winced and covered his face with one hand. He used the other hand to point at one of the doors in the back of the large space.

Clint was thrown off by the inside of the place. It didn't just look like a barn on the outside—it felt like a barn on the inside, as well. That made the shabby walls sectioning off the lower floor into rooms seem even more peculiar. Before he asked about which room he needed to go to, Clint saw the door on the left rattle in its frame.

"They were on their way out when they started shooting," the clerk said from behind his desk. "They just fired and ran back inside."

"Is there any law around here?"

"No."

"Then stay out of my way," Clint said as he ducked his head and ran toward the room.

The clerk disappeared from sight, but his voice drifted through the air like something from a squeaky fiddle. "They got Marta! Don't shoot her!"

But Clint had enough on his plate without conversing with the clerk. Before he reached the door, he saw it open a bit so someone inside the room could peek outside. Clint was able to take another step or two before the door was thrown wide open to show Sarah filling up a good portion of the doorway.

"Howdy, Clint!" she shouted as she fired a shot from a rifle that she held near her hip.

Clint thanked his lucky stars that Sarah had taken her shot so quickly. The bullet hissed through the air and snagged his shirt on the left side near his ribs as it went by. He managed to fire off a shot of his own while leaping to one side, but he felt pain bite through his stitched wound at the same time his other arm hit the wall. The Colt barked once and blasted out a chunk of the door.

Stepping straight back into her room, Sarah levered another round into her rifle and brought it up to rest against her shoulder. "Come on in, Clint! I've got something real nice for you."

Clint knew that she would be expecting him to work his way to the door and try to get inside. He hoped she wasn't expecting him to run straight into the barrel of a loaded rifle, because that's exactly what he did. When his foot stomped against the floor outside the door, a shot from the rifle punched through the wood. Before another round could be levered into the chamber, Clint was busting the door down with his shoulder.

Sarah was inside the large room, fumbling with the rifle as Clint came in. She turned on the balls of her feet and rushed toward the back of the room, laughing merrily as she raced across the floor. Her clothes were rumpled and her red hair flew around her face in a messy tangle.

But Clint wasn't interested in how Sarah looked. His eyes were drawn to a large window at the back of the room. The window was halfway open and a cold breeze rushed in between fluttering curtains. It was a large picture window that went all the way down to below waist level, giving Clint a real good look at the terrified woman being pressed against the upper pane.

"Better not get much closer," Sarah warned. "I think Jonas has got an itch in his trigger finger."

Clint froze when he saw Jonas standing behind the woman. He gripped her by the back of the neck and repeatedly slammed her face against the glass. Whenever the woman screamed or winced, Creed smiled a bit wider.

"Come on outside with me," Creed said.

Sarah did as she was told and ducked to fit through the window after swinging one leg up and over the sill. Since the window was tall enough to display the top of Creed's head, Sarah didn't have any trouble getting through it without opening it any wider. Once she was outside, Sarah ran away and was out of Clint's sight.

"You're Clint Adams?" Creed snarled.

Clint could barely hear the words through the glass and over the woman's occasional screaming, but Creed's voice was like an icy blade that cut through everything else.

"Yeah," Clint said. "That's me. I'm putting my gun down. Just let the woman go."

Creed's mouth hung open a bit and his eyes followed the motion of Clint's hand as he placed his Colt on the floor. With his smile still in place, Creed looked like he was winded after running for a mile, but still captivated by something even farther away.

Clint straightened up and held both hands where Creed could see them. "There. My gun's down. Let her go and I'll let you ride away."

"Who else is with you?" Creed asked.

The woman clenched her eyes shut and started to cry, but was silenced when Creed gripped her neck tighter and cracked her forehead against the window.

"Answer me!" Creed demanded.

"It's just me," Clint replied.

Creed glanced through the window as if he was expecting more men to rush into the room with Clint. When none arrived, he shrugged and said, "Too bad. It's gonna take a lot more than you to bring me back."

With that, Creed's smirk turned into a wolfish grin as he pulled his trigger and blew a hole through the woman's head while also shattering the upper portion of the window.

THIRTY-FIVE

The gunshot rolled through Clint's ears as if he'd been the one to catch that bullet. When he saw the woman's face turn into a lifeless mask, Clint knew he would be carrying that sight with him for a long time to come. Dropping to one knee so he could scoop up his Colt, he set his sights upon the window and broke into a run.

Clint might not have known who that woman was, but he'd be damned if he was going to let Jonas Creed get away with murdering her in cold blood.

More shots were fired through the window as well as into the surrounding wall, but Clint wasn't going to be distracted so easily. When he reached the window, Clint turned his body so his left shoulder hit the pane at the same time as the elbow of the arm he held out to protect his face. The remains of the glass fell away easily and the window's frame splintered on impact to let Clint pass.

Even before Clint's boots touched the ground outside the window, he was firing the modified Colt. There wasn't much behind the hotel, so it was easy for him to spot the two people running away from it. Unfortunately, Creed and Sarah weren't the only two people in the area.

Sarah ran as quickly as she could without turning around

to watch where she was going. While trotting backward, she aimed quickly and fired at Clint. Her bullet punched through the wall of the hotel behind him.

Creed wasn't as concerned with Clint. Instead, he made a beeline across the lot behind the hotel and lunged for the closest bystander he could find. Creed's hand was outstretched as Clint fired a bullet that ripped through his forearm.

For a second, Clint wasn't even sure he'd hit Creed. There was a fine spray of blood, but Creed barely even twitched at getting hit. Before Clint could fire again, he saw Creed grab a young man wearing bib overalls and swing the man around so he could duck behind him.

"You already got one lady killed!" Creed shouted. "You want more to end up the same way?" With that, Creed raised his pistol and fired a quick round into the young man.

Hollering in pain, the man in the overalls doubled over and flopped onto the ground. Sarah knocked a heel against him as she kept backing up and then turned to hop over the wounded man while she fought with the rifle's lever.

Clint gritted his teeth and aimed his Colt as if he were simply pointing his finger at Creed's chest. Somewhere during the split second it took for Clint to pull his trigger, Creed staggered to one side as if the ground had tilted beneath him. The Colt bucked against Clint's palm, but didn't do anything to slow Creed down.

"Run along now, Clint!" Sarah shouted as she tossed a quick wave over her shoulder.

Clint brought up his Colt and was ready to fire. Sarah was running toward a pair of outhouses at the edge of the hotel's back lot and she held her rifle in both hands. At the last second, she changed directions to rush toward the front of the outhouses instead of behind them.

Clint could have fired a shot, but his only target was Sarah's back. It was a target he wouldn't have missed, but pulling his trigger at that moment went against his grain so much that it made him realize what an animal felt when its fur was rubbed the wrong way. Clint pushed aside his reservations in a matter of seconds, but that was more than enough time for Sarah to find another form of cover.

Creed circled around the outhouses and ran straight for a group of horses tied to a nearby post. Without batting an eye, he took aim at a trio of women clustered behind the shop next to the hotel.

"Let him go or he dies!" Sarah shouted.

Shifting his eyes toward her, Clint found Sarah standing next to a man who had bolted from one of the outhouses. She had the barrel of her rifle wedged against the man's ribs.

Clint didn't even wait for her to say a word. Figuring she was going to shoot no matter what, he took aim and sent a round through the crook of Sarah's arm. He hit the meat near her elbow, which caused her to drop the rifle before she could fire. Clint doubted she would have had the strength to pull her trigger even if she could have kept the rifle from falling.

Letting out a scream that was equal parts anger and pain, Sarah ran to catch up with Creed.

Following her while also trying to keep track of Creed, Clint spotted movement from the corner of his eye. He felt some relief, knowing that the movement came from the man in overalls who was now trying to get the hell away from there. Still reluctant to shoot a woman in the back, Clint fired a quick shot at Creed.

Pulling away the first set of reins he could reach, Creed dragged a light tan Palomino from where it had been hitched and climbed into the saddle. All the while, he fired shot after shot in Clint's direction.

Clint dropped to one knee as all that lead came flying at him. Once Creed was in his saddle, he clamped the reins between his teeth and filled his other hand with a second pistol. Within moments, there were enough bullets whipping through the air to hit Clint at least once if he stood his ground. Rather than try to take his chances dodging all those rounds, Clint rolled backward and then pushed off with one leg to roll to one side.

It took every bit of restraint Clint had to keep from pulling his trigger. The only thing holding him back was the knowledge that only one live bullet remained in his cylinder. Clint picked out his target again, ignored the hot lead that was still screaming around him, and fired his last shot.

Creed's upper body jerked once, but he still managed to pull Sarah up behind him and ride away.

THIRTY-SIX

Solomon was practically jumping out of his skin when Clint rushed back to the spot where he and Heather were waiting. The first thing Clint made sure of was that Heather was still in control of him. Since they'd struck their arrangement, Clint had allowed Solomon to ride without his arms and legs tied. He'd also given Heather his holdout pistol in case things got too rough. Heather acknowledged Clint's glance by showing him the small pistol she kept in one hand.

"We saw what happened!" Solomon said. "I'll stay here and you can collect me later."

Clint walked over to Eclipse, ignoring the impatient way that Solomon was waving toward the Darley Arabian.

"Well, go on!" Solomon urged. "Go after them."

After reloading his Colt, Clint grabbed ahold of the saddle horn and lowered his head. "We're not going after them. Not right away."

"What?" When he didn't get a response from Clint right away, Solomon blinked and looked around as if he were waiting for someone else to back him up. Since Heather wasn't about to step in, he looked back at Clint and grunted, "*What?*"

"You probably didn't see what happened from back here, but you had to have heard the shooting," Clint said. "There were just as many shots fired at me as there were at folks who just happened to be standing nearby. I knew those two were crazy, but . . ."

"Rozekiel ain't a saloon!" Solomon said. "It's where loons like Creed belong and he needs to get back there."

"Loons? Isn't that the pot calling the kettle black?" Clint mused.

Solomon ran over to grab Clint's arm. His hand was immediately shaken loose, but Solomon kept pressing. "Creed's not right in the head. I may not be, either, but Creed will kill anyone and everyone he don't think is on his side. Whether I'm riding with you or not, just being out of his sight for so long means my head's on the chopping block too! The longer I stay away from Rozekiel, even the goddamn law will figure I was out raising hell with them other two. They got to be stopped one way or the other, Adams!"

Snapping his head around to glare at Solomon, Clint asked, "You don't think I know that? You think I'm content to just let them ride off? Creed and Sarah both started off by dumping Heather from a horse to trip me up, and now they've moved to shooting innocent folks just to distract me from coming after them. What the hell do you think they'll do next if I just keep coming after them?"

"So you just want to let them go? That sounds like the words of a damned cr—"

Solomon was stopped by a gentle hand that fell onto his shoulder. Although the touch was soft, there was more than enough strength in Heather's grip to catch Solomon's attention.

"Just stop right there," she said. "Both of you, take a breath and don't say anything to make things worse." Even though she was talking to both men, her last comment was definitely aimed at Solomon. "Clint's right. Those two will just keep killing if they feel threatened. Jonas needs to tire himself out and when he does, Sarah will ease back as well."

"I'm giving them a good enough head start to get away from this town as well as any homes that may be nearby," Clint announced. "As soon as they're clear, I'm going to finish what was started here."

Heather turned her eyes toward Clint. "No," she said sternly. "That's not what we should do."

"What did you just say?"

Heather's voice remained strong despite Clint's gruff tone. "You heard what I said," she told him. "This isn't the first fit Jonas has thrown and it's not the first time he's hurt people along the way."

"You call this a fit?"

"It doesn't matter what I call it," she insisted. "Jonas is known to get violent and it takes him a while to cool down. If you try to approach him again so soon, he'll be just as bad as he was now . . . if not worse."

"Not if he doesn't see me coming," Clint pointed out. "And if we're in the open, it doesn't matter how big of a fit he wants to throw."

Heather looked at Clint with eyes that were surprisingly calm, and her voice had yet to show the first sign of fear or worry. "Can you guarantee he won't see you coming? Or that Sarah won't see you coming?" Before Clint could reply, she quickly asked, "And how can you be so sure nobody else will be around when you find him?"

Clint was still riled up, but he forced himself to take a breath and consider what Heather had said. Once her words sank in, he had to admit, "I can't guarantee any of those things, but letting him get too far ahead of us is dangerous. Are you certain we should wait?"

"If you're not going to trust me on something like this, why did you even let me come along?"

Clint was quiet for a second, which was enough time for Solomon to speak up. "She's got you there," he said.

Nodding, Clint said, "I guess she does. I won't spark another fight right away, but I can't let Creed stumble upon some other folks when he's got the taste of fresh blood in his mouth. What happened to Grant's family won't happen to anyone else. Not by that animal's hand."

"Agreed," Heather said. "I can stay back here to watch over Solomon."

"No," Clint told her. "You're coming with me. Both of you are."

"Both of us?" Solomon asked cheerfully.

Clint smirked and said, "Don't look so happy about it. Things may get real bad real quick and I don't want to have to take the time to think about where you may be."

THIRTY-SEVEN

Within minutes, Clint, Heather, and Solomon were on their horses and racing out of town. Clint felt as if he were leaving a place that had just gotten hit by a twister, since the whole town was a chaotic mess after all the shooting that had taken place. As much as Clint hated to just ride away from that mess, he knew it was the best thing he could do in order to prevent even bigger messes from forming.

Having seen which way Creed rode out of town, Clint was able to pick up his trail fairly quickly. Since Creed wasn't exactly concerned with sneaking about, Clint's task was that much easier. While finding Creed wasn't too big of a challenge, figuring out what to do from there wasn't exactly easy.

Creed's trail led Clint to a short stretch of houses that had been built outside of town. To find the two fugitives, all Clint really needed to do was follow the sounds of chaos. In the few spots where he might have needed to climb down from his saddle and check for actual tracks, Clint simply had to sit still and listen for the sounds of screams and gunfire. Thankfully, he heard more of the latter than the former.

"I see them!" Solomon shouted loud enough to be heard

over the rumble of hooves against the ground. "Last house on the left!"

Clint looked at the house, which was first in the short row of homes. He recognized Creed's horse moments before he spotted the two figures struggling to pull someone out of the house. When he pulled back on his reins, Clint held out an arm to make sure Heather did the same.

"Stay back here," Clint said. "We don't want to force their hand again." With that, Clint reflexively reached for the rifle that was normally holstered in the boot of his saddle. The rifle wasn't there. Come to think of it, Clint was pretty certain that rifle was the one Sarah had been firing at him not too long ago.

Drawing his Colt, Clint shook his reins a bit, which was just enough to get Eclipse to start walking slowly forward. Clint had to hold himself back from rushing straight toward the houses, but that didn't mean he was content to sit and do nothing. He knew he was a bit outside of the Colt's range, but Clint aimed at the house and pulled his trigger a few times anyway.

The shots weren't accurate, but they didn't need to be. Clint was, after all, firing at the broad side of a house. One round punched through a spot near the roof and the other shattered a side window. Seconds later, the door swung open and people bolted outside as quickly as their legs would carry them.

The first few people must have been residents or neighbors, because they obviously weren't Sarah or Creed. They ran outside and headed straight for the next house. Not far behind them were the two figures that Clint had been waiting to see.

"Back up," Clint said as he pulled back on his reins to do the same.

Heather moved back and wound up directly beside Eclipse.

Creed emerged from the house with a gun in each hand. He turned wildly about to look around as Sarah came outside as well. When Creed pointed toward the neighbor's house, Clint fired another few shots well over their heads.

Although Clint couldn't make out what Creed was saying, he could tell the fugitive had spotted him. Clint rode forward a few paces and prepared to fire another few warning shots.

"No," Solomon snapped. "He's gonna go for his horse. Just give him a second."

Clint held his fire. He intended on giving Creed a second, but no more than that.

Sure enough, Creed headed for his horse as he pointed both guns at Clint and pulled his triggers. Even though Clint knew he was outside of pistol range, he pulled back hard enough on Eclipse's reins to get the Darley Arabian to rear up and pump his front legs into the air.

The show must have been impressive from a distance, because Creed let out a wild holler and emptied both pistols. Sarah shouted at Clint as if she'd won a prize and brought the rifle up to her shoulder.

"Go!" Clint shouted.

Heather brought her mare all the way around as Clint directed Eclipse to follow suit once he was back on all fours. A rifle shot cracked through the air and was followed by another in the time it took for Sarah to work the lever.

Clint only rode a few yards before turning Eclipse around and heading back. "They're making a run for it," he said as he watched Creed race for the trees behind the houses. "And it doesn't look like he's got anyone with him."

"That was real good!" Solomon said. "Especially that last part. You really looked like you got chased off."

Clint shrugged and replied, "We were out of pistol range, not rifle range."

Solomon's face paled a bit at that, but he nodded and kept his mouth shut.

Snapping his reins, Clint rode down the small hill that led to the houses. Heather kept pace with him just fine as he reined Eclipse to a stop between the two houses where Creed had made his stand.

"Is everyone all right?" Clint asked.

Of the seven or eight folks who were milling around, only two of them were composed enough to speak. "They just came here and kicked the door in!" a young woman with short, braided hair told him. "They didn't even say what they wanted."

"Is everyone all right?" Clint asked sternly.

"Yes. Ellie was slapped around a few times but—"

"Was anyone killed?"

"No," she replied, flinching at the urgency in Clint's voice.

"Did they take anyone with them? Was anyone kidnapped?"

The woman looked around and did a quick count. "No," she said before long. "We're all here. We just—"

"Go inside and lock your doors," Clint told them. "If you have guns, keep them ready. If you see that man or that woman come anywhere near here again, shoot first and sort the rest out later."

With that, Clint snapped his reins and tapped his heels to Eclipse's sides. Creed's trail was still fresh and Clint wasn't about to let it cool down.

THIRTY-EIGHT

Creed kept heading north. No matter how many sharp turns he would make for what seemed like no reason at all, he would always get his nose pointed north again and then move along. Fortunately, the only things that could be seen in that direction were bare trees and snow-capped mountains.

The sun fell below the horizon early and left a cold chill in the air. When he lifted his nose to the wind, Clint pulled in half a breath and frowned. "It's going to snow soon," he said.

Heather had already wrapped a shawl around her shoulders, which she now pulled even tighter around her.

Solomon rode behind Clint and lifted his face even higher, as if he wanted to sniff the air above the section that Clint had just pulled in. "I don't know about snow, but it sure as hell is gonna frost tonight. I hope Creed picks a place that's nice and warm."

"He's not going to have much choice," Clint said. "There's not another town along this trail for miles. Even if he whipped that horse within an inch of its life, he wouldn't be able to get anywhere near a bed tonight."

"He's going to be upset," Heather said. When she saw

the puzzled look that Solomon tossed over his shoulder, she added, "More upset than before, I mean."

Clint smirked and shifted in his saddle. He'd only lost sight of Creed a handful of times throughout the day. Thanks to the high terrain and the absence of any leaves on most of the branches on either side of the trail, Clint could keep the fugitives in his sight more often than not. When Creed did ride behind some evergreens or around a bend, Clint only had to pick up the pace for a bit and keep his eyes open to catch sight of him again.

Without an audience to frighten or innocents to terrorize, Jonas Creed didn't have many other tricks up his sleeve.

"How was Creed brought in to Rozekiel?" Clint asked.

"You mean, how was he captured?" Heather replied.

"Yeah."

"He was found inside a house full of bodies. From what I hear, it was very gruesome."

"I heard all about it," Solomon chimed in. "Several times, in fact. *Gruesome* ain't the word. At least, not for how Creed describes it."

"He just runs out of steam or gets bored," Clint mused.

Heather nodded to herself. "I suppose that should make it easy to catch him."

Clint turned around to look at her. "I don't think he gets bored with me around."

Although she looked like she was inclined to agree with him, Heather didn't say anything to that effect.

"Don't fret too much," Clint said as he shifted back around to face forward. "Have you ever had to hunt a wild dog?"

"No," Heather replied.

Solomon started to laugh. "I shot my dog when he went mad. Turns out he just stuck his snout into a jug of my aunt's soap."

Ignoring that, Clint said, "A wild dog will snap at any-thing that's in front of him and he'll keep snapping until he kills it. When he's left alone, the dog will walk real slow and real quiet. He'll even curl up into a contented ball and go to sleep. If anything wakes him up, though, he'll go right for its throat."

"You could always shoot it from a distance," Heather suggested. Her voice was tired and the words themselves sounded like they hurt her when she'd spoken them.

Clint ignored those words just as he'd ignored Solomon's dog story. "If a wild dog runs for too long and tastes too much blood, you can't just walk up to it with a gun and expect it to just stand there and take the bullet. Sometimes they do, but sometimes they prove to be even nastier when they're cornered. Those kinds of dogs need to just get their wildness out and slow down on their own. Once it gets tired or too sick to keep its head up, it'll curl up and wait for the bullet. I doubt it wants to die, but it knows what's coming."

"Kind of like rabbit hunting," Solomon said. "When I was a kid, I chased rabbits down all day long. Whenever they'd stop to rest, I'd stomp the ground and get them run-ning again. I'd find 'em and keep it up until they couldn't run no more. When they got tired enough, I could just walk up and do whatever I wanted. Like once I took a hammer—"

"You still have that gun I gave you?" Clint asked.

Heather chuckled nervously and replied, "Yes."

"Good. Keep a close watch on the rabbit hunter."

THIRTY-NINE

After following Creed for so long, Clint felt as if he knew where the fugitive wanted to go before Creed even got the thought in his own head. Clint kept his spyglass in one hand to check in on Creed every so often during the night. He spotted the opening to a cave that was almost entirely covered by dead trees and fallen branches. A minute or so later, Creed steered his horse in that direction.

"All right," Clint said as he motioned for Heather to bring her mare to a stop. "This is where you two stay."

"But I think Creed is still moving," Solomon said.

"He's headed for a cave. That's where he's going to spend the night."

Solomon strained his neck to look around Clint. "I think he's still moving."

"Then I'll follow him myself," Clint replied. "Or I could just wait for him in that cave. If he doesn't like the open sky over him when he sleeps, that cave's his only real option. That is, unless he wraps himself up in a blanket."

"One of the orderlies at Rozekiel tried to get Jonas to do that," Heather said. "Jonas kicked out almost all of the boy's teeth."

Solomon let out a short, grunting laugh. "I remember that one."

"Just stay here," Clint snapped. "Keep your heads down and stay quiet. If I'm not back in an hour, Heather, take Solomon back to Rozekiel. If he puts up a stink . . . shoot him."

The tone in Clint's voice hit Solomon like a punch in the stomach. When he glanced over to Heather, he noticed she already had her gun in hand.

"I could go with you," Solomon offered.

Clint flicked his reins to get Eclipse moving again. "No, thanks," he replied.

In the minutes that followed, Clint lost sight of Creed for longer than at any other time during the day. While that would have made him hurry to catch up to the fugitive earlier, Clint wasn't worried about it now. Everything he knew about Creed made Clint certain that he didn't need to look any farther than that cave. At that moment, it was as if the madman had somehow intended to lead Clint to that very spot all along.

Some folks might have called that kind of thing instinct.

Clint thought of it as knowing his prey.

The path to the cave was a wooded slope that was broken up by several boulders and clusters of small rocks that jutted out from the ground. More than once, he considered tying Eclipse to a tree and sparing the Darley Arabian the rest of the trip, but the stallion pulled through just fine. Clint dismounted a few paces from the mouth of the cave and looped Eclipse's reins around some branches. That was enough for the stallion to stay put and wait for Clint to return.

Approaching the cave at an angle, Clint was able to watch for movement near the opening. He could already tell that several of the branches in the vicinity had been recently snapped and the dirt outside the cave was covered in fresh tracks. He was in the right spot, but that didn't make Clint feel any better.

His ears strained to pick up a sound. Anything from a boot scraping against rock or someone coughing inside the cave would have been noticed. Clint was preparing himself to be ambushed or shot at with every step. Part of him was even expecting to be surprised. As odd as that may have been, he knew he had to be ready for anything at all where Creed was concerned.

Hearing nothing at all grated against Clint's nerves like a rake against dry slate. When he got close enough to hear the faint echo of wind within the cave, Clint would have been happy to hear a gunshot or anything else to move along the fight that he knew was coming.

Clint kept still for almost a minute, waiting to hear any sound made by either of the fugitives. When he didn't even hear anything from Creed's horse, he began to wonder if his knowledge of his prey was correct after all. Whether his instinct was right or not, he knew he would have to go into that cave.

Creed may have been crazy, but he wasn't crazy enough to just walk out with his hands held up and beg for mercy. And since Creed also wasn't deaf, he'd surely heard Eclipse scrambling toward the cave a while ago.

Clint knew Creed was in there. All that remained was for him to go in and drag Creed out again.

As he approached the cave and prepared to step into the almost complete darkness within, Clint felt like he was the crazy one.

FORTY

The opening to the cave was about five feet tall and almost twice as wide. Clint had his gun out and aimed into the shadows as he ducked his head and looked inside. Even before his eyes adjusted to the darkness, he could pick out the shape of a horse several yards inside the cave. When he eased himself in a little farther, Clint's hat and shoulders scraped noisily against the dead branches that hung down from the top of the opening.

Clint squinted and was soon able to pick out a few more blocky shapes in the shadows. The cave looked like it went in quite a ways, but there was no way for him to know how far. He wasn't about to charge forward and find out, however. That would have been foolish considering the fact that he could now make out the shape of someone crouched less than five paces in front of him.

Both Clint and the figure ahead of him remained still. Soon, Clint's ears picked up one of the sounds he'd been so anxious to hear. It was a low, strained breath that was pushed out after being held for just a bit too long. Clint kept his gun aimed at the source of that breath as he stepped inside the cave. Stepping to one side, he glanced left and right to make sure there was nobody standing beside him. Although there were thick shadows within that cave, he could tell there was nobody standing anywhere close to him.

"I could kill you right now," Sarah said after she'd let out her breath and pulled in another.

"You had plenty of chances," Clint reminded her. "Since you didn't take those chances, why not come along with me now?"

"Go along to where? Back to that sanitarium?"

"It's time. This has gone on too long. Too many people have been hurt."

"I know," Sarah said in a trembling voice. She took a step toward Clint and into just enough light from the outside to show the rifle in her hands. "Soon as you're dead, this'll all be over."

Clint heard another breath, but this one didn't come from Sarah. It was a wheezing chuckle that came from Clint's immediate left. It also came from down low, which explained why he hadn't seen the figure that had been so close all that time.

Letting out a sound that was close to an animal's snarl, Creed reached out from where he'd been hunkered down against the cave's wall. His legs were curled up beneath his body and his head hung low to make him look more like a rock than a man in the darkness. He grabbed for Clint's legs, but Clint was already stepping away from him.

Rather than try to get farther away from Creed, Clint changed direction and lowered his shoulder so he could pin Creed against the rock wall. His move took Sarah by surprise as well, because she fired a shot into the spot where Clint would have been if he had jumped out of Creed's reach.

The rifle's muzzle flash illuminated Sarah's face for a second, displaying a quick glimpse of a face that was contorted into a violent sneer. As Creed fought to get out from where he'd been trapped, Clint aimed beneath the flash of the rifle and fired a shot.

Sarah let out a pained scream and hit the dirt. The heavy thump of the rifle came at the same time, letting Clint know that the weapon wasn't aimed at him for the time being.

The shadows were working in Creed's favor. He pulled at Clint's arm and leg. When he couldn't get a good hold on him from there, Creed tugged at Clint's clothes until Clint had no choice but to drop down and be turned around by Creed's insistent, flailing grabs.

Clint could feel Creed's fingers clawing at him and snagging in his clothes. Since he couldn't see where the man's hands were, he could only react when another one took hold of him. When he felt the touch of iron against his chest, Clint strained every muscle in his body to twist and lean away from it.

The pistol barked once and lit up that corner of the cave for a split second. In that second, Clint saw Creed's wild eyes and leering face. He also felt the burning from the sparks that exploded from the gun's barrel. The warm trickle of blood ran down Clint's stomach, but he didn't allow himself to think about that right now. To stop moving at this point would have been the end of him.

Creed fired his gun again, but it was only after Clint had grabbed that hand and shoved it away from him. The sparks flew away from both men and sent a bullet to ricochet farther into the cave. Clint tightened his grip around Creed's wrist and then pulled Creed's gun hand closer to him.

Creed's reflex was to try to pull his arm back. When Clint felt that, he shifted his own muscles to push in that same direction. With Creed pulling his arm and Clint pushing it, Creed's gun hand sped toward the cave wall and slammed against the unforgiving rock. Creed let out a pained grunt, but didn't loosen his hold on his gun.

Even though Clint's eyes were as adjusted to the dark as they were going to get, he could still barely see what he was doing. One of his hands held his Colt and the other was wrapped around Creed's wrist. Since he couldn't see much of anything anyway, Clint tossed his gun toward the cave's opening so he could grab Creed's shirt and drag him along the wall. Creed kicked and flailed, but he wasn't in much of a position to do anything else.

Clint could hear Sarah scrambling to get to her feet. He knew she was tightening her grip around the rifle and probably looking for a good target. Clint could tell Creed was about to right himself enough to gain some leverage and fight properly. Before that could happen, Clint gathered all his strength and threw Creed out of the cave.

Even as Creed hit the ground and rolled for a few more feet, Clint dove for his pistol and picked up the Colt in one pass. Rolling onto his side, he aimed into the cave and fired a shot that sparked against the stone ceiling and bounced around amid a series of loud pings. He hoped that would keep Sarah back for a few seconds as he dealt with the greater of the two evils.

FORTY-ONE

"Did you hear that?" Solomon asked. "Those were gun-shots!"

Heather stood with her back against her mare's ribs so she could keep constant watch on Solomon. She held the pistol in both hands to keep it steady at all times. "I heard it."

"We should help him."

"No," Heather replied sternly. "Clint told us to stay here. He knew there was going to be a fight and we shouldn't go in and confuse things."

"Confuse things? He could be dead right now."

When Solomon walked toward her, Heather tightened her grip on the pistol. The gun was fairly small, but it weighed her arms down like an anchor. "If he's hurt, we'll—"

"We'll be next and you know it," Solomon snarled as he rushed toward her.

Heather reacted by bringing up the gun to point it at him. Her arms were halfway up and a warning was on the tip of her tongue when Solomon got to her. Before she realized she was in trouble, Solomon had ahold of her pistol and was pulling it away from her.

"Give me that gun," he snapped.

"Get back. We're waiting right here."

Solomon spoke through gritted teeth and he continued to pull at the gun in Heather's hands. "I already waited long enough and now's just the time I been waiting for. Give me this pistol before you get hurt."

Once the surprise had worn off, Heather fell back on some of the things she'd picked up during the years of dealing with wild-eyed men like Solomon Reyes and Jonas Creed. She kept her hands on her weapon and brought her knee up to pound into Solomon's groin.

Now it was Solomon's turn to be surprised. He reflexively pulled in a breath and braced himself against Heather's knee. Her aim was a bit high, so her blow caught Solomon more in the lower abdomen instead of the spot where it had been aimed. That victory was short-lived, however, as Heather dropped that leg straight down so she could slam her heel into his shin.

As Solomon reeled back in agony, his grip loosened enough for Heather to pull away from him with the gun still in her possession. Before she got too far away from him, Solomon lashed out with one hand to slap her across the face.

The back of his hand hit her flush, but she rolled with the impact and staggered away from him while hanging on to her gun.

"Give me the pistol," Solomon demanded.

Heather's mouth was set into a grim line. Her eyes were focused intently upon him. "I won't give you this gun, Solomon. You're staying here and that's final. Clint doesn't need our help."

"That's a hoot," Solomon chuckled. "First off, he's probably already dead. And second, I don't give a shit about helping him anyways. All I want is to get the hell away from here."

"You're staying here."

Solomon studied her with cold, twitching eyes. His gaze

lingered on the blond hair that flowed over her shoulder and then drifted down to the curve of her breasts. "You know how many of us boys at Rozekiel wanted to get you alone? And it weren't just the crazies, either. I heard a few doctors swapping stories about you. Were any of them true?"

"Get over here and stay put," Heather said firmly. "I'm warning you."

"You're a nurse, lady. You ain't no killer."

Heather placed her thumb on the pistol's hammer and pulled it back. "This has gone too far. I can't allow you to roam free. Come back here and then we'll go back to the sanitarium."

"I'm goin' where I please, lady. As for you . . . you can go straight to hell." As he said that, Solomon began to run for the trail that led away from the cave. He was stopped in his tracks when Heather fired a shot that whipped only a few inches over his head.

"I don't want to shoot again," she warned. "Please don't make me."

Solomon looked over his shoulder at her. Even though he was clearly rattled by the last shot, he was quickly regaining his confidence. "You ain't gonna do anything but fire over my head. Without that gunman around to protect you, I'll come after you and kill you with my bare hands. That is, unless you can drop me with your next shot." Grinning, he added, "And I can see you ain't about to do that."

More gunshots echoed from the cave and the sounds of a struggle could be heard. When Heather looked in that direction, she was drawn back to the sight of Solomon making another run for his freedom. She fired once more and was able to clip him with a grazing shot.

"God damn it!" Solomon growled. "That hurt!" He patted his side and found a fresh scratch that wasn't much deeper than if someone's fingernails had done the damage.

"I warned you," Heather said.

By this point, she could see Clint and Jonas fighting outside the cave. It was an ugly display of two men simply doing whatever they needed to do in order to stay alive. There was no finesse or strategy to be seen. In the few seconds that Heather could watch it, the fight looked more like two wildcats rolling in the dirt and slashing at each other.

Solomon was watching as well. The sight of what was happening outside that cave was more than enough to light a fire under him. Turning his sights toward Edie, he said, "I'm taking that horse and getting the hell out of here."

"No, you're not," Heather said as she planted her feet and took aim with the pistol in her hand. Even as Solomon stomped toward her, she made sure to place herself between him and the brown mare.

"Step away from that horse or I'll hurt you!"

"You're going back to Rozekiel," she said. "That's all there is to it."

"Fine, then," Solomon said with a cold edge in his voice. He clenched his fists and stalked toward her. "Sorry I got to do this."

"Me too," Heather replied.

Solomon's steps quickened as he rushed the slender blonde. After that, a single gunshot erupted between them.

FORTY-TWO

More than anything, Clint knew he had to keep ahold of his gun. With Creed tearing at him like a crazed animal, that one task was going to be a whole lot harder than it sounded. After every punch Clint landed, Creed rolled to one side and landed one of his own. The blows Creed landed came in a random order and from a different direction every time.

While Clint tried to place his punches in good spots, Creed would just hit any part of Clint he could reach. While Clint tried to buy himself some time or distance so he could fire his gun, Creed was just punching or kicking to inflict damage wherever he could.

The madman's fists never ran out of steam. Even the punches he landed that didn't hurt Clint right away were piled up one on top of another until Clint felt like he could barely stand up. Creed pulled him down and threw him to one side so he could slam his boot heel into Clint's arms or ribs before unleashing another flurry of punches.

Finally, Clint had to block out the pain and force himself to see through the fog that all those punches and kicks were pushing into his head. He stopped trying to guess what Creed was going to do next and stopped trying to think of a way to get the upper hand. Instead of all that, Clint simply pulled himself along as if he were fighting his way through a storm.

He lowered his head, braced himself for the inevitable pain he would feel, and just tried to set his mind upon one simple goal.

Clint struggled to get off the ground. He then tried to get ahold of Creed's throat. Once Clint did those things and leaned back far enough to aim his gun at Creed's face, the chaotic fight was over.

Both men could barely pull in a breath. They were bleeding from their noses. Their eyes were blackened and several large knots were swelling up to the size of fists upon their faces. Clint felt pain every time he moved, but he kept pushing it down to the back of his mind. Now that he'd managed to pin Creed to the ground, he wasn't about to waste the opportunity that presented itself.

Clint wedged the barrel of his Colt under Creed's chin and pushed upward until Creed was forced to stare straight up at the clear night sky.

To anyone else, the sight would have been beautiful. Some might have called it tranquil. The tree branches swayed in the breeze and didn't have any leaves to block the sight of the inky black sky that was studded with hundreds of thousands of glittering stars.

For Creed, the sight was almost unbearable. He squirmed and kicked and slapped his hands against the ground as he tried desperately to roll onto his stomach or twist his head away. Clint grabbed Creed's face and held it in place. Even though the barrel of the Colt wasn't frightening Creed in the least, it was a solid piece of iron that did a good job of keeping Creed's head pressed against the ground.

"No!" Creed shouted. "I'll fall off! I'll fall off, God damn you!"

Clint's instinct was to talk to Creed or even ask what was going through the madman's head. He pushed those instincts down, since Creed was quickly losing his steam. Seeing Sarah emerge from the cave, Clint looked over to her and said, "Get back in that cave or I'll kill him!"

Sarah let out a panicked shriek and scuttled back into the shadows.

When Clint looked down at Creed, he saw tears streaming down the man's face. Since Creed was barely struggling any longer, Clint moved the gun out from under his chin, but kept it ready.

Breathing in labored gasps, Creed couldn't seem to pull his eyes away from the sky. "I'm gonna fall off this damn world and keep falling up there."

Clint had heard of folks getting nervous when they were out in the open for too long, but never something like this. He wasn't about to question it, however, because whatever demons Creed had were doing a good job of quieting him down now.

"I'm taking you back to Rozekiel," Clint said. "That's where you belong."

Slowly, Creed nodded. "They'll . . . probably drill more holes in me."

Clint ignored that. He figured it was just more babbling. Then he caught sight of the small circular scars along the sides of Creed's head. In the pale moonlight, the scars almost seemed like pennies that had been melted onto his scalp. "What holes?" Clint asked.

"The ones in my head," Creed said. "They're supposed . . . supposed to let out the blood clots or water or whatever's in my head. It sure worked," he added with a tired chuckle. "I recall plenty of blood coming out when they drilled into me."

"Then maybe I'll just take you to jail," Clint told him. "Either way, you're going to answer for what you've done."

Creed's voice was tired as he sighed. "Yeah. Just so long as I can lay down somewhere."

Clint wasn't about to let his guard down. Even though Creed seemed to be too tired to do anything but grumble to himself, Clint wasn't going to assume the fight was over. He kept his gun in hand and aimed in Creed's direction as he slowly got to his feet and stood up. With the Colt still aimed at Creed, Clint reached down to grab hold of Creed's collar.

"Come on," Clint said as he lifted Creed off the ground. "Get up and we'll get going. We've got a long—"

Without one bit of warning, Creed clamped both hands around Clint's wrist and twisted until the Colt was no longer aiming at him. From there, Creed sunk his fingernails into Clint's wrist and then buried his teeth into the meat of Clint's hand.

Clint tried to step back and pull his hand away, but that only helped Creed pull himself up and onto both feet. Resisting the urge to hit the side of Creed's face or anywhere else that might cause him to tear away a large hunk of his hand, Clint snapped his knee up into Creed's gut.

That impact made Creed's jaw slacken a bit, so Clint followed it up with another knee to the same spot. As soon as Creed pulled his head back, Clint pulled his hand free and took a few steps back as well.

"Here, sweetie!" Sarah yelled as she tossed Creed's gun through the air.

Clint saw the pistol sailing toward Creed's hand and immediately made a move of his own. He picked out his target and figured his angles in less than a second. Clint then raised his gun arm and took aim, but felt pain stabbing from the bite in his hand as well as the newly opened stitches in his shoulder. Even with all that, Clint squeezed his trigger and sent a bullet toward the gun that was arcing down to Creed's outstretched hand.

The bullet hissed through the air, missing the pistol by a fraction of an inch.

Catching the pistol and then shifting his grip to place his finger on the trigger, Creed grinned viciously as he aimed at Clint.

The second bullet from Clint's modified Colt was slightly off target as well, but still caught Creed in the chest and knocked him off his feet.

Even as he fell over, Creed still fired two shots from the pistol that Sarah had tossed him. He landed on his back with his eyes wide and filled with terror as he spent his last few moments looking up at the open sky that stretched out above him.

Clint looked over at Sarah, but didn't aim his gun at her. He was too tired to make any more threats or swap any more insults with her. Instead, he simply told her, "Don't make me chase after you."

Either Sarah was too tired to run or she didn't like what she saw in Clint's eyes because she fell to her knees and curled up into a ball against the edge of the cave's opening.

FORTY-THREE

Clint rode back up the trail with Creed draped across the Darley Arabian's back and Sarah trailing along tied to the saddle of Creed's horse. When he reached Heather, he found her tying Solomon up as best she could. Solomon didn't put up much of a fight, which brought the wound in Solomon's leg to his attention.

"What happened to him?" Clint asked.

Heather sounded almost as tired as Clint when she replied, "He tried to get away so I shot him. I think his knee is shattered."

"Oh. Are you ready to head back?"

"Yes. I want to go home."

"Me too," Solomon groaned.

Clint and Heather both glanced at him and said, "Shut up!"

Solomon did as he was told and was in too much pain from where he'd been shot to try anything during the ride back to Rozekiel. Sarah spoke up a few times along the way, but Clint put a stop to that by stuffing a bandanna in her mouth.

Clint rode up the path that led to Rozekiel's front gate with Heather riding beside him. What struck him so odd about the place was the fact that it seemed just as quiet and orderly as the first time he'd ridden up to it. Patrick even came rushing out to greet them.

"You're back, Heather!" the boy said cheerfully.

She nodded warily and said, "Yes, I am. Could you get Dr. Wolcott please?"

The boy nodded and hurried to the front door of the main house. By the time Clint had reached the entrance and swung down from his saddle, both Dr. Wolcott and Dr. Liam were rushing outside.

"Mr. Adams!" Wolcott exclaimed. "It's so good to see you again. I see you found Sarah and Mr. Reyes. Excellent!"

"Creed's here, too," Clint said.

Dr. Liam had gone over to help Sarah down from the saddle and had spotted Creed's body strapped across the horse's back. "Is he . . . ?"

"Yeah," Clint said. "And so are some other folks in another town he and Sarah ripped through."

Dr. Wolcott shook his head. "It's a shame you couldn't put him down before he did so much damage."

Wheeling around to face Dr. Wolcott, Clint asked, "Put him down? You mean like a dog?"

"Well . . . if he was going to kill innocent people . . ."

"I was trying to bring him back alive. If you'd wanted him dead, you or one of your orderlies could have just put a gun to his head and pulled the trigger! Or would you have preferred to drill into his skull?"

Dr. Wolcott blinked and sputtered for a few seconds before he collected himself enough to say, "I am not an executioner, Mr. Adams."

"And neither am I."

"As for the drilling, well, it's an experimental procedure."

Clint looked back and forth between the two doctors. "Procedure? You mean like they used to do in the Dark

Ages to let the demons out of folks' heads? That sort of procedure?"

"Of course not!" Dr. Wolcott said. "That's ridiculous. There's evidence that blood or other fluids can build up in the brain and create enough pressure within a patient's skull to create delusions or cause erratic behavior."

"So you drill holes to let it out?"

Although Dr. Wolcott obviously saw where Clint was going with that, he couldn't exactly refute the point being made. "It's a controlled procedure," Dr. Wolcott explained. "And the results have been favorable."

"Well," Clint said as he looked over at Solomon, "that one tried to wring Heather's neck and take her gun away so he could do God knows what to her. And Sarah shot a few people for no other reason than to make noise. There's some erratic behavior for you."

"I'll take note of that," Dr. Wolcott said. "Thank you very much. I have some procedures in mind that are somewhat radical, but should prove useful in ending such violent outbursts."

Some burly orderlies had already come out to take Sarah and Solomon back into Rozekiel. Judging by the panic written across both of their faces, the two patients were already imagining the procedures that Dr. Wolcott would consider radical.

"There's a reward coming to you," Dr. Liam said. "We truly do appreciate your help, Mr. Adams."

"Great. Whatever the reward is, send it to me in town."

FORTY-FOUR

After leaving Rozekiel, Clint rode into Running Springs and rented the first room he could get that was on the side of town farthest from the sanitarium. It was a small room, but the bed was soft and it had a fireplace that was plenty big enough to warm every corner.

Clint sat in a chair with his shirt off, facing the fire. Although the heat from the flames felt good against his skin, that wasn't the reason he'd stripped off his shirt. He was reminded of that reason when a needle punctured the flesh in his shoulder and pulled a thread all the way through.

"After all the things that damn wound's been through, you'd think I'd be used to that by now," he grumbled.

Heather sat in a chair next to him. Her long blond hair was pulled back into a single braid to keep it out of her face as she worked to stitch him up. "Maybe you wouldn't have needed to get it stitched again if you would have just let it heal properly."

"Creed wasn't so considerate in that regard."

"I know." She ran her hand along Clint's shoulder as she worked the needle. "It sounds terrible, but after seeing all that blood and death, part of me just hoped you would have shot him and been done with it."

"If it wasn't for this damn wound, I could have done just that," Clint told her. "Any other man would have been dead long before things got so bad. But Creed . . . he's not exactly any other man. The only way an animal like that could get any worse was if he was wounded. I needed a clean shot and before I could get one, Sarah would always come along to—"

He was cut short by a gentle hand upon his mouth. Once Clint had stopped talking, Heather rubbed his cheek and continued with her stitching.

"You don't have to explain yourself," she said. "I was there. You did the best you could. Creed got his way at Rozekiel because most other men would get too spooked to deal with him after he had one of his bad spells. It was probably one of those frightened men who slipped up enough to let Creed and those others get away."

"Were the rest of the patients rounded up?" Clint asked.

"Yes. Marshal Laherty was awfully proud that he and his deputies could catch a bunch of patients who were too petrified of their own shadows or Lord knows what else once they got outside. One of the deputies will be dropping off your reward sometime soon, by the way. I wouldn't expect a formal thank-you or anything else so civil."

"I wasn't expecting one. Your bosses gave me all the civility I could stomach."

Heather sighed and cinched up the last stitch. "Those doctors aren't my bosses anymore. I suppose I don't have any bosses at the moment."

"Why? Are you leaving Rozekiel?"

"I told Dr. Liam as much as soon as you rode away from there. When I was working there, I thought I was doing some good. I thought I'd help folks get better and tend to them when they were sick. At that place, I wasn't much more than a jailer. Sometimes, I felt like I was just feeding animals and cleaning their cages. Does that make me terrible?"

Clint shifted so he was facing Heather directly. "You couldn't be terrible if you tried. From what I've seen, you did nothing but help those people. You sure helped me. I couldn't have brought in those three without you."

"Thanks for saying that," Heather replied as she put on a tired smile. "But I think you would have done just fine without someone else to watch over."

"You took care of Solomon. If you weren't there, he would have just waited to get closer to Creed and all three of them would have ambushed me at once. You also told me what would shake Creed up enough to get the edge on him. With my gun arm hurting, I needed every advantage I could get."

Patting his arm gently, Heather said, "Speaking of that, you need to rest this and let it heal properly. How long did those stitches last?"

"I felt them tear when Creed and the rest of them busted out of Rozekiel," Clint admitted. "Dr. Wolcott did a real good job of getting that lead out of me, though."

"You should be good as new soon, but only if you rest up."

"See?" Clint said. "You were born to be a nurse. It'd be a shame to give that up."

"I know. I just need to get away from this place. There are some doctors where I got my schooling who have always said they'd keep a spot open for me if I ever came back. It's time to take them up on that offer."

"Dr. Wolcott probably didn't like hearing that."

"He sure didn't," Heather replied. "But all I've seen lately is blood and murder and . . . well . . . Rozekiel isn't the sort of place anyone should stay for too long if they can help it."

"Since I've been ordered to take it easy for a while, I could accompany you for a nice ride to . . . wherever you're going."

"I wouldn't want to inconvenience you, Clint."

"What inconvenience? I was planning on refusing that reward money, but I could take it and use it to pay for our expenses. That is, unless you intend on going through rough country or getting into a mess of trouble along the way."

She laughed for a few seconds and then allowed herself to relax more than she had for quite a while. "I don't plan on getting into any trouble, and you are definitely taking that money. You earned it."

"Then it's a deal," Clint said. "We can put this place behind us and use Marshal Laherty's money to pay for some comfortable rooms along the way."

Just then, Heather reached out to gently unbuckle Clint's belt.

"What are you doing?" he asked.

"Just relax," she replied as she moved her hands down to unbutton his pants. "We wouldn't want to break those stitches."

FORTY-FIVE

Heather's hands moved so quickly and gently that Clint barely even felt them. Before he knew it, he was sitting in his chair having his jeans eased off him.

"This is a surprise," he said.

Heather smiled and unbuttoned the front of her dress. "I hope it's a good one."

"Sure, I just thought you weren't feeling very well."

"I wasn't, but that was before. After all that's happened, I need something good to balance out everything else." Once the top of her dress was unbuttoned, she eased it off her shoulders and then let it drop to her feet. Stepping out of the fallen garment, she kicked it away and straddled Clint's lap. "This is the best thing I could imagine right about now."

Holding on to her hips and watching as Heather shook her hair free from its braid, he said, "I'll second that."

Heather's body was slender and pale. It was clear she spent most of her time inside, since she didn't even have any calluses on her hands. As she straddled Clint while he leaned back in his chair, Heather ran her fingertips down along Clint's chest. By the time her hands made it to his waist, her own nipples were erect and begging for Clint's attention.

Unable to hold himself back, Clint wrapped an arm

around her and pulled her closer so he could place his mouth on her and taste her skin. When his tongue found her nipples, she pulled in an excited breath and wrapped both arms around him.

"That feels so good," she whispered.

Clint ran his tongue between her breasts until he was looking up into her eyes. "I've just gotten started."

"Me too." With that, Heather reached down to guide Clint's rigid penis between her legs. Once she felt him part the moist lips of her pussy, she lowered herself onto him until she'd taken most of his length inside. Heather sighed contentedly and trembled with anticipation as she felt him grow a bit harder while inside her. Soon, she started to rock back and forth in his lap.

Clint kept one hand pressed against the small of her back and let the other wander up and down along the curve of her spine. Heather's trim body moved gracefully on him and every so often she would let a contented sigh escape her lips. When she leaned forward, her soft blond hair brushed against Clint's shoulder and tickled his back.

Heather's body moved a bit faster as she started to pump her hips with urgency. Leaning back, she put her hands flat upon Clint's chest and closed her eyes while riding his cock in a steady rhythm. Clint put his hands on her hips and felt the muscles working in her lower body. The moment she slowed down, he cupped her firm backside and stood up from the chair.

Her eyes snapped open in surprise and she held on to him as if she were about to be tossed to the floor. When she realized she was just being carried over to the bed, Heather closed her eyes again and enjoyed the ride.

The bed was covered by a thick quilt, which Heather nestled into the moment Clint set her down. She lay back and he positioned himself on top of her, but waited before doing anything more than that.

Opening her legs for him, Heather said, "Don't keep me waiting, Clint. Please."

He couldn't have waited any longer even if he'd wanted to. Clint reached down to feel the downy, golden hair between Heather's legs. When he slid into her again, he savored the way her tight little pussy wrapped around him. The deeper he plunged into her, the more Heather sighed. Her sigh turned into a trembling moan once Clint began to slide in and out with a rhythm of his own.

Heather's hair splayed out on the bed under her and her back arched against the mattress. Her breasts may have been small, but they were a perfect fit for her slender figure. As Clint continued to thrust between her legs, she closed her eyes and ran her fingers along her erect nipples. Clint caressed the side of her body and watched as she writhed with the pleasure that was building inside her.

Clint watched the changes in her face as he touched her in different places or changed the power of his thrusts. Just when Heather started to relax, his hands would find a new spot to make her squirm and moan all over again. Before too long, he felt her body shake and heard her breath catch in the back of her throat.

Clint ran his fingers through her hair and kissed Heather powerfully on the lips. When he pumped into her again, she let out a gasp that went directly into Clint's mouth. She followed that by slipping her tongue between his lips and kissing him with renewed passion.

Heather's hips wriggled in time to Clint's thrusts and she wrapped both legs around him. Running her hands along Clint's back, she kept kissing him as Clint pumped in and out between her legs. When she finally leaned her head back, Heather pulled in a breath as if she'd been under water for the last few minutes. Even after she'd filled her lungs, she continued to gasp and claw at Clint's back.

She started to say something, but her next breath was

taken from her as a powerful orgasm rippled through her entire body. Even Clint could feel her climax as nearly every one of her muscles tensed and her grip upon him tightened for several seconds before she even started to let him go. Just as she seemed to regain her senses, Clint took them away again by driving into her again and again.

"You said you wanted something good," Clint whispered. "Did you find what you were after?"

"Yes," she gasped. "God, yes. And if you keep it up, I'll find it again."

Watch for

LOUISIANA SHOOT-OUT

322nd novel in the exciting GUNSMITH series
from Jove

Coming in October!

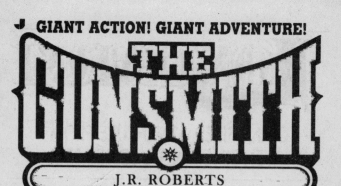

GIANT ACTION! GIANT ADVENTURE!

THE GUNSMITH

J.R. ROBERTS

Little Sureshot And
The Wild West Show
(Gunsmith Giant #9)

Dead Weight
(Gunsmith Giant #10)

Red Mountain
(Gunsmith Giant #11)

The Knights of Misery
(Gunsmith Giant #12)

The Marshal from Paris
(Gunsmith Giant #13)

penguin.com

M228AS0608

GIANT-SIZED ADVENTURE FROM
AVENGING ANGEL LONGARM.

BY TABOR EVANS

2006 Giant Edition:
LONGARM AND THE
OUTLAW EMPRESS

2007 Giant Edition:
LONGARM AND THE
GOLDEN EAGLE SHOOT-OUT

2008 Giant Edition:
LONGARM AND THE
VALLEY OF SKULLS

penguin.com

M240AS0508

DON'T MISS A YEAR OF

Slocum Giant
by
Jake Logan

Slocum Giant 2004:
Slocum in the Secret Service

Slocum Giant 2005:
Slocum and the Larcenous Lady

Slocum Giant 2006:
Slocum and the Hanging Horse

Slocum Giant 2007:
Slocum and the Celestial Bones

penguin.com

M230AS1207

AUG -- 2020

Penguin Group (USA) Online

What will you be reading tomorrow?

Tom Clancy, Patricia Cornwell, W.E.B. Griffin,
Nora Roberts, William Gibson, Robin Cook,
Brian Jacques, Catherine Coulter, Stephen King,
Dean Koontz, Ken Follett, Clive Cussler,
Eric Jerome Dickey, John Sandford,
Terry McMillan, Sue Monk Kidd, Amy Tan,
John Berendt...

You'll find them all at
penguin.com

*Read excerpts and newsletters,
find tour schedules and reading group guides,
and enter contests.*

Subscribe to Penguin Group (USA) newsletters
and get an exclusive inside look
at exciting new titles and the authors you love
long before everyone else does.

PENGUIN GROUP (USA)
us.penguingroup.com

M224G1107